KISS
of the LION

Kiss of the Lion

by

Susan E Westoby

Pharaoh Press

Kiss of the Lion
ISBN 0 9525543 2 1

First Published in 1996 by Pharaoh Press, Roby, L36

Produced by NEMO,
Woolton, Liverpool, L25 7RE

Printed in England by Cromwell Press,
Wiltshire

Cover illustration by John Kirvan

Dedicated to the beautiful
Elly May Pickstock
With Love

Time

Across a room our eyes met,
Like yesterday it seemed and yet,
You briefly spoke — I could not say
What I'd rehearsed for days and days.
You kissed my cheek, my heart did race,
To feel your lips upon my face.
The moment passed, now it's too late
I love you still, but time won't wait.

Jenny Martin

CHAPTER I

Guido Velucci did not want to die.

But if he did not find money, a lot of money from somewhere and soon, then his body may just be found floating, tangled in the reeds of the River Arno one fine morning.

He moved forward to join the throngs of Florentine lords crowding the steps of the Duomo, waiting to greet the French King Charles VIII as he and his forces entered the city of Florence. The Medici had fled before them and the nobility of Florence were glad to see the back of their former rulers, welcoming the French with open arms.

Guido grimaced as he was jostled rudely. Then he turned pale as a familiar voice hissed in his ear. "Two days! You have two days, Monsignor, to settle your debts. Remember!"

Although he turned his head quickly, the whisperer had gone, but Guido knew who it was, knew who had breathed the threat. Piero del Aguila, servant of the Borgias, executioner, debt collector, procurer of women. Del Aguila turned his hand to most things to keep his master happy. Guido's entrails turned to water for he knew what would happen once those two days were up if he had not found the money which he owed to the Borgia. Two days! He was certainly a dead man!

An irresistible surge of those about him carried Guido forward as the long introductions and speeches of welcome to the French, began. On the balconies of the Palazzo Velucci, Guido's ancestral home which directly overlooked the Piazza del Duomo, there was also a jostling and a shoving and pushing. It was an indication of the almost hysterical excitement which gripped the butterfly ladies of the House of Guido Velucci.

Of Guido's six daughters, Valentina was the youngest but also the most determined. With many a sly pinch and sharp jab of the elbow, she finally succeeded in finding a most gratifying vantage point from which to view the pageant that was the vanguard of the French army.

"Madonna! They are so many. No wonder the

Medici fled in such haste."

Her laugh trilled high and she tossed back her hair and leaned out all the more for a better view of the colourful throng below her. A startled horse reared. A quick command in French and a glinting lion's glance made Valentina catch her breath for a moment before the cavalcade had moved on and all she could see was a flurry as the Frenchman endeavoured to control his mount in the close packed lines of warriors.

Suddenly, strangely, the laughter died in Valentina's throat and her stomach convulsed and cramped in inexplicable panic. She was saved by her mother who had to catch hold of her daughter's arm to drag her away from staring after where the Frenchman was still trying to control his horse.

"Enough of this! Daughters come inside at once. We must prepare for the arrival of our guests." Bianca Velucci stressed the last word a little ironically. She could not understand how her fellow Florentines could welcome a foreign King with so much enthusiasm. However, being the wife of Guido Velucci, she kept her mouth shut and her opinions firmly to herself.

With downcast eyes and a not too convincing attempt at modesty, the six daughters of Guido and

Bianca Velucci trooped inside after their mother. Medina, the eldest, then Lucrezia and Cara, the twins and Bianchetta, Francesca and finally, Valentina.

"Oof!" Bianchetta turned on her young sister angrily as Valentina cannoned into her. "Watch out, clumsy one."

A mumbled apology made her stare. The expected response would have been a cheeky challenge but Valentina's mind seemed to be elsewhere.

The excitement almost reached fever pitch as servants scurried to and fro lighting the thousands of candles which were set to illuminate the Palazzo Velucci in such a way as to hide the peeling colours and threadbare furnishings of a House, once proud and immeasurably rich but now brought low by its Signor's addiction to gaming and foolhardy trading ventures.

Guido Velucci bemoaned his lack of luck and blamed his misfortune on villainous and unscrupulous partners but if the truth be told it was his own greed and mis-management which had caused his downfall. To add to his troubles his wife had not even produced a son and heir, but six girl children for whom, if he was to get them off his hands, he would need to provide dowries. An impossibility which, at times, made him suicidal.

Now, though, there was a certain anticipation in the air, an expectation of a change of fortune, for the all-powerful Medici had left Florence. With the arrival of the French came fresh opportunities, fresh blood, perhaps, to ally with the Velucci. Guido was hoping that they would be bringing fresh money with them also. If his life was to continue beyond the next forty-eight hours then he must clutch at any straw.

"Make sure the daughters are at their best." He instructed his wife. "If we miss this opportunity to marry one or two of them off then you may need to start making arrangements for a funeral."

Bianca pulled a sour face behind her husband's back. She did not know exactly what it was that he was involved in but she knew that it was connected with the Borgias and she could well believe that his life might be in danger.

Their only chance may be to find a rich husband amongst the French for one of their daughters and that would not be an easy task. It was with this in mind, therefore, that all available hands had been set to stitching and embroidery in an attempt to provide finery for as many of the Velucci daughters as was possible.

As the youngest, Valentina, unfortunately, was the last to acquire anything vaguely wearable. Her mother sighed as she inspected this, the last of her daughters. "Well, there is nothing for it. You must stay out of the way. At least you are young enough for us to take a little more time to find you a husband. Whereas Medina..."

Valentina's eldest sister was twenty-three years of age and classed as a despairing spinster in Florentine society. Lacking a rich dowry, she had the further misfortune to take after their father in looks and temperament. Dark and heavy brows met over close set eyes which rarely sparked with humour. Spite turned down the corners of a mean mouth and a fine dark down decorated her upper lip.

Dear Lord, if she was expected to wait until Medina was married, then she may as well take Holy Vows now, Valentina thought gloomily.

There was nothing for it except to bow to the inevitable and being of a generous, warm-hearted nature, she did her best to help her sisters to get ready, although in the process she suffered many a slap and sly pinch as nerves were stretched and tempers frayed. Finally Valentina was left, alone, as her mother and sisters swept down to the great hall with both their colour, and their expectations, high.

When peace and quiet had settled after the hysteria and chaos, Valentina occupied herself for a while with picking up and sorting what was left of ribbons and material, threads and pins. When all was tidied away she wrapped what remained of some crimson silk about her shoulders and she pirouetted and simpered and curtsied before the huge gilded mirror set against the wall of the room she shared with Bianchetta and Francesca. After a while, even that simple entertainment palled and Valentina sat down on the floor amidst the heap of discarded materials.

Inevitably she thought of him. That French lord's presence intruded into her solitude in spite of her irritable attempt to dismiss him. She shivered, as though she had escaped by a hairs' breadth, some dreadful fate.

Then her stomach growled and she was relieved to turn her mind to her need for food, something which had been forgotten in all the excitement of helping her sisters. She would have to go down to the kitchens herself, for every available servant was helping with the banquet provided for the French lords. It was no hardship for her for she often sought sanctuary near the heat of the vast fires which burned day and night, providing the food for the family Velucci.

This time it was like entering hell.

The heat, the noise, the milling bodies, the smell, almost blasted Valentina off her feet, but eventually she was able to purloin a few pieces of chicken and some ciabatta bread and with her spoils wrapped in a cloth she escaped from the inferno to seek a quiet place to satisfy her appetite.

The Palazzo Velucci had been a most splendid construction in its day, with spiralling galleries and beautifully frescoed ceilings, gold leaf and entrancing statuary. Now, except for the main hall and one or two rooms on the lower floors kept in use for appearances' sake, the greater part of her home was crumbling, dusty and unused. Valentina's favourite hideaway was in that unused part of what had been a minstrels' gallery, overlooking the main hall but discreetly hidden by mouldering velvet hangings. She knew that she could watch what was going on without being seen and she could enjoy her picnic in privacy.

The dust up here was thick and cobwebs clung to the high wooden panelling. Valentina blinked as she pulled aside the moth-eaten hangings and slipped through onto the gallery. Her wide, excited gaze took in the brightly lit, sparkling scene below and with a sigh of delight she slid down to the floor with her back against the carved balustrade and unwrapped her food. Almost, she was too entranced to eat, but her healthy young appetite would not be denied for long and she tucked in hungrily while her avid gaze sought faces, familiar and foreign, in the glittering throng below her.

Guido and Bianca Velucci sat at the top of the great long table set with gold platters, eating utensils and candlesticks, all borrowed from friends in order not shame the House of Velucci. The French captains were ranged on either side of them with the Velucci daughters strategically placed amongst the most important of the French lords.

Thousands of candles reflected on the glittering jewels, not only on the arms and fingers, round the necks and in the ears and hair of the women, but also on the fingers and round the necks of the men. The heavy scent of various perfumes cloyed the air and as the wine flowed, laughter rose and women became less discreet, leaning towards the admiring male glances and displaying creamy bosoms and smooth shoulders for their delight.

Valentina finished her food and wiped her fingers

clean, but continued to crouch in her hiding place entranced by the glittering sight which seemed to embody all her youthful dreams. Her eager eyes picked out those she knew, then she turned her attention to the French. There were six of the French lords seated at the table of Guido Velucci and Valentina was a little disappointed at their age and appearance, having expected men of heroic proportions in these conquering lords.

One figure only, the Frenchman seated to the left of her father, held her attention. A faint prickle of terror raised the hairs on the back of her neck although she told herself scathingly that there was no reason to fear anyone here in the safety of her father's house.

He was younger than the others, not too much older than herself, she calculated and he had a languid grace as he lounged in his chair. One leg was hooked over the arm, swinging gently and his cup was lazily held in careless fingers. He raised the cup to his lips and his eyes wandered away from the chattering, laughing throng around him in an idle inspection of the palazzo's main hall.

All at once he seemed to freeze, holding himself as still as if mesmerised and Valentina's throat closed, a sweat of panic breaking out on her upper lip. For one wild, lunatic instant she thought he looked straight at her, kneeling concealed in the dark shadows of the old gallery. For several moments they were entrapped thus, then a breath of relief left her lungs as that foot started to swing again and he leaned forward to place his cup on the table before him.

She watched him for a while longer as he leaned towards her father to speak in his ear, but she did not notice her father's start of surprise, then his frown as he listened to the French lord, because she was too busy admiring the cut of the young Frenchman's doublet where it emphasised the width of his shoulders. A collar of rubies which caught the light and glittered like fresh blood against the burgundy velvet of his doublet bore witness to a well-lined purse. His hair was very dark but it gleamed with fiery lights under the candles, its thick lustre emphasised by the straight cut above level brows.

Valentina could not see the colour of his eyes from where she knelt, but they were certainly not dark as were her own, dark as fathomless pools and fringed with long curling lashes which could flutter down expertly to hide her expression when it was needful.

Tearing her eyes away from him at last to enjoy the antics of some tumblers entertaining the company, she finally sighed and forced her cramped limbs to move, edging backwards out of her hiding place. A last glance towards the table brought a pang of disappointment as she saw that the place where the Frenchman had been sitting, next to her father, was now empty.

Gingerly Valentina groped for the curtain behind her, catching hold of its edges with a faint sense of relief and easing herself silently out into the passageway. It was only as she turned that she realised with a shock that the formerly gloomy corridor was now almost as brightly lit as the hall below and her heart sank as she faced her father.

Guido Velucci's face was purple with rage and for one hysterical moment Valentina imagined him bursting with anger here before her. She forced down that almost irresistible urge to giggle.

"'Tis my youngest daughter, Monsignor." Guido could scarcely force the words through his clenched teeth.

"Daughter!" The amused tone of the Frenchman's voice only served to increase her father's anger. "I thought her some serving maid, crouching in the dark to spy on us."

The husky sound of that voice drew her gaze and her heart leapt in panic as she realised that it was he whose horse she had frightened earlier that day.

A sudden movement made Valentina dodge away to avoid Guido's fist, raised to punish her for embarrassing him in front of his guest.

The blow, however, never fell. Powerful white fingers closed like a vice around her father's wrist and Valentina's eyes were drawn like a magnet back to the Frenchman. She was suddenly, whirlingly lost in that now strangely desired, lion-gold gaze. The colour surged up into her face and her breath caught suffocatingly in her throat at the lazy sensuality which gleamed at the back of those eyes.

"Now, now, Monseigneur, surely you would not wish to mar the market value of such a beautiful face in one brief unthinking moment of anger. If 'tis true that this is one of your daughters then I am sure that if you and I were to discuss the situation, we might find something to our mutual advantage..?"

The voice trailed away on a significant uplifted note and Valentina was left bewildered, unable to grasp the meaning of the words, yet relieved at their effect on her father. The startling engorged colour left his face and his muscles slackened as he relaxed into thought, rubbing his right wrist, which had now been released, almost absentmindedly as he slowly nodded his head.

"Yes, yes of course." He laughed oddly, a touch of excitement in his face. "You are quite right, Signore de Baisleon. Daughter, go back to your room and I shall speak to you in the morning."

Guido could never remember his daughters' names easily. Valentina sighed a breath of relief at being let off so lightly and glanced up gratefully at the Frenchman. He smiled and all those whirlwind reactions to him came storming back, shaking her, confusing her again.

He gestured to her father to precede him. "You are an understanding father, Monseigneur, and I am sure the Lady..?" A brow quirked in her direction.

"V-V-Valentina." She forced the word through dry lips as her tongue refused to obey her will and she grew angry with herself at her response to him.

"Yes. I am sure the Lady Valentina knows that you have only her interest at heart."

Guido laughed again with that undercurrent of excitement.

"Of course. Of course. Only her interests at heart."

They turned away together and Valentina curtsied at a point somewhere between the two of them and waited until she was once more alone in the corridor. In the darkness. Alone and strangely forlorn.

Valentina turned to walk slowly back to her room, her legs shaking. The safe haven of her bedchamber welcomed her and she closed the door softly and moved over to lay down on the bed, staring up into the gloom of the tapestried bedposts.

When she pictured his face, heard again that soft accented voice, she experienced a churning sensation in the pit of her stomach which was both strange and delightful. Wondering if he was one of those who would be staying at the palazzo, she hugged herself on a surge of terrified anticipation then groaned as the door opened and Bianchetta and Francesca fell giggling into the room, full of the happenings of the evening, of flirting and laughter and the possibilities of a match with a French husband

Guido Velucci rubbed his hands together and almost chortled with glee. The last thing he had expected was an offer for his youngest daughter, and what an incredible offer the young fool had made! Only think, Guido had almost kept her hidden away because he had not been able to dress her decently. Well, enough of struggling now. Not only could he pay off all his debts but there would be plenty left for generous dowries for his other daughters. Enough to buy strong alliances, influential friends.

He was saved. Saved from the threats of the Borgia. It would give him great pleasure to throw the money in the face of that insolent dog, Piero del Aguila and he would make sure that he never fell into the clutches of the Spaniard again.

Hunching his bony backside into bed next to his long-suffering wife, he grasped her by the shoulder pushing her onto her back.

"Money! Sets the juices flowing again, eh?"

"But she is so young..." A faint protest, for her last born, stifled at her husband's frown.

"Old enough! And we cannot afford to worry. The Frenchman is soft on her to the point of obsession. It is the best we could have thought of for her. Now – open your legs."

CHAPTER II

Valentina was awoken next morning, not by the little maid whose duty it was to wait on the three younger sisters, but by her mother, Bianca Velucci. Bianca was in a strange mood as she snatched back the heavy shutters and allowed the sunlight to pour in and pick out the shabbiness of the furnishings.

"Come, daughters, stir yourselves. This is a most important day."

Valentina struggled to clear the fog of sleep from her brain. "Mama. What is it? What is happening?"

Normally, none of her daughters would dare to question her, but Bianca answered briskly.

"A wedding."

"A wedding?"

"How wonderful!"

17

"Has someone offered for Medina?"

"Was it one of the French lords?"

The questions now came thick and fast from the three young women who tumbled from the bed and searched for clothing cast away so carelessly the night before.

"It is not Medina."

That silenced them. Something about the stance of their mother's stout figure made them uneasy.

"Then who?" Francesca and Bianchetta glanced at each other.

Valentina had the most awful premonition. She knew what her mother was going to say before she spoke the one word.

"Valentina."

There was a gasp of disbelief. Valentina's two sisters stared at her, first in awe, then jealously.

"But she's only a baby."

"What did Medina say?"

"Enough! We must hurry. Your father is waiting for us."

Valentina, herself, stood like a statue. Confusion and disbelief fought for supremacy within her breast. Who could possibly have offered for her? She had met no man who could be termed eligible and anyway, what of Medina? She tried to question her mother but was whirled and twirled about like a rag doll, her stammered attempts at speech ignored until finally she was dressed and brushed and readied to meet whoever it was that was to be her husband.

As she followed her mother down to the salon where Guido Velucci awaited them, she heard her sisters whispering behind her and when the three older girls joined them those whispers became loud enough for her to hear.

"But who could it be?"

"Some purblind fool who likes young flesh."

"I am glad it is not I. Imagine some old man – wrinkled flesh – ugh!"

The comments wound up her nerves until she was so scared that she suddenly, desperately needed to relieve herself.

"Mama!" She tried to attract her mother's attention to no avail. A hand pressed to her stomach helped but she was so concerned that when they all finally came to a halt Valentina almost cannoned into her mother's back.

A soft, half-smothered laugh drew her eyes to the figure leaning against one of the heavy, carved chairs and as her huge-eyed stare met the amusement in the lazy golden eyes of the

Frenchman her bladder almost emptied itself on the spot. Deaf to what her father was saying, it was only when an expectant silence finally settled that she realised they were all waiting for her to reply.

Sweet Jesus, what was she supposed to say? She had not even heard a question.

Stuttering and stammering, trying to bluff her way through, he took pity on her and came to her rescue.

"Indeed, Demoiselle, your joy and delight are exceeded only by my own." His italian was fair but not fluent. "I know you will forgive the haste in the ceremonies but you must be aware that my King and his forces leave for Rome soon. Thus the need for us to be wed before we depart."

She missed the slight inflexion of sarcasm which threaded his voice as indignation brought a return of her usual courage and made her protest. "But that is impossible Signore! I do not even know you. How could you possibly want to marry me?"

Then she cowered back at the sudden movement from her father as he lunged towards her. Guido Velucci was not about to lose a fortune because of a mere girl's reluctance.

His daughter was no longer within reach of his punishment, however, for Valentina had been caught in what seemed to be a band of steel which took her shoulders in a protective embrace and spun her away from Guido's attack. Pressed, trembling against the lean strength of the Frenchman's side, she watched her father pull up short under a menacing lion's stare and grow pale at the deadly snarl of the French captain's warning.

"Beware! Monseigneur Velucci! The girl is promised and paid for, and no-one... no-one threatens what is mine!"

Velucci threw up his hands placatingly and tried to smile, effecting a rictus grin which twisted his features alarmingly.

"I wanted only to convince her of the need for haste. My wife spoils the daughters and sometimes I have to apply a firm hand..."

"I am sure that you do," a thread of silk now in that voice as it soothed the Florentine and invited his confidence. "However, her discipline will now be in my hands and I can certainly take care of my own."

Valentina could scarcely breathe, he held her so tightly, yet she felt suddenly safe as though she was where she belonged. His talk of discipline did not frighten her.

Guido was so relieved that he had been able to

divert the anger of the young man before him, whose very pores oozed a threat to those who would cross him and he turned to his wife, signalling frantically with his eyes for her to take the girl away and indicating to the Frenchman a tray holding wine and goblets. "Shall we drink to our bargain then my dear Captain, whilst the ladies make themselves ready for the ceremony?"

Valentina's mother gentled her daughter away from the embrace of the Frenchman although she had had some difficulty in doing so. It seemed he was reluctant to let go.

"I am sure you must be eager to take your bride away and become... acquainted with her." A slight pause, then a rush of words as a dark brow raised in enquiry. "A happy event, Monsignore, which I am sure will bring blessings to both sides."

"Yes. An hundred thousand ducats' worth of blessings."

Guido ignored the open sarcasm and handed his guest a goblet of wine, raising his own cup in salute before drinking deeply. Raoul de Baisleon sipped at his own drink, watching the Florentine consideringly over the rim of his cup.

Why he had offered so much for Valentina he did not know. He had the feeling that he need not have proposed marriage to get her. This man was so desperate for money he was sure that he could have had the daughter anyway, with her great dark eyes and raven's wing hair. What then had brought on this rush to bind himself in wedlock at his age, a state which he had hitherto been fortunate enough to evade in spite of many a plotting mother at the French court?

With a slight shrug of those powerful shoulders he dismissed the questions from his brain. It was time he got himself an heir anyway, and one female was as good as another. At least this one had a dark beauty which certainly stirred his blood, although he suffered a slight twinge of disquiet at the memory of the flash in her eyes when she had protested at the haste of the marriage, then he firmly turned his thoughts to preparations for his wedding and the subsequent departure for Rome.

In Valentina's room a sense of panic prevailed. Not only were the Velucci daughters' maids pressed into service but Valentina's sisters themselves were forced to turn their hands to packing and pressing and arranging hair. A dress for Valentina had to be found and the only one likely to be suitable was a yellow silk which had to be forced out of her sister Lucia.

Lucia was the only one who was the same height as Valentina but she was much stouter and so the dress had to be hastily altered. It did not suit her slim frame and olive complexion. The neckline gaped and was fastened with a cloak brooch, the best they could do. Finally, after much screeching, spitefulness and loss of temper, especially on the part of Medina, who was furious that her youngest sister was to be married before her, they were ready.

Their mother's familiar warning, "Hurry. Your father will become impatient." Ensured a flurry of haste although accompanied by sulky sighs and venomous glances at Valentina, the object of so much fuss. Valentina herself was silent throughout the whole ordeal. It was true that she would have had no choosing of her husband under normal circumstances but at least she would have been allowed some time to get to know any prospective bridegroom. All this frantic rush frightened her.

Francesca tried to liven Valentina up a little with some optimistic comments on life with the French court but her only response was a nod or a vague smile until even she lapsed into silence. When all was as ready as it could be under the circumstances, they trooped down to the small family chapel where the wedding was to take place.

Bianca made an attempt to reassure her daughter. "This captain is highly trusted by the French King, although he is so young and he seems gentle and considerate. Generous too." Bianca had been astounded at the sum the Frenchman was prepared to pay for her daughter, a little worried also. "Now remember. Just try and relax. Do as he says and I am certain it will go easy for you. There will be some pain at first but it is nothing. Soon over." If only she had had more time to give advice, instruction. Valentina knew nothing. Too late now.

The doors to the chapel opened to reveal Guido Velucci and the men of his House and, to the right of the small altar, the French captain dressed superbly in dark green velvet, a chain of matched emeralds across his breast. Their brilliance was only rivalled by the golden gleam of his eyes as he turned to watch his bride approach him.

Valentina experienced a deep sense of shame at the state of her own attire. The yellow silk dress had so obviously belonged to someone else of more generous proportions and she was bare of any jewels except for a simple gold crucifix which encircled her slender throat and gleamed between her breasts.

Francesca had done her best with her hair but in

the flurry of the preparations and with no jewels nor ornaments to support it, already the glossy, thick tresses were slipping from their elaborate coils. Valentina lowered her eyes, unable to face the splendid figure of the man who would soon be her husband.

Everything had happened so fast. One moment she was the youngest daughter, last on the list for marriage opportunities, not even worthy of dressing up to greet the French guests, the next she was the centre of attention – being married off to a total stranger and preparing to leave her family within a matter of days.

The marriage ceremony stood out in her mind as a shameful ordeal. Aware of the scarecrow figure she cut next to her husband's magnificence and confused and upset by the suddenness of it all, she stammered badly over the responses required of her. She did not usually stutter so but the fact was that Valentina was in shock, hardly understanding what was happening to her.

Then, as her father gave her hand into the strong, warm clasp of her husband and his fingers gripped hers in hard reassurance, she felt the confidence surge back. Her voice regained its strength and she finished her vows, strong and clear. All eyes watched as the French captain turned his new wife towards him. He hesitated for a fraction of a second then his head descended and Valentina's senses spun in an arc of fire at the demand in his lips and the wild response which shook her body sent her arms up to clasp those wide shoulders in an almost feverish embrace.

Time suddenly held no meaning for the two of them holding each other so closely there until the embarrassed clearing of a throat and a faint laugh vaguely penetrated the fog of passion which held them. Valentina was the first to pull away although her new husband was most reluctant to let her go.

Eventually, however, he was persuaded and he turned her to present her to his countrymen, who delighted in the opportunity to kiss the young bride and to exchange ribald jokes and comments with the groom. Valentina's family stood silently to one side until finally the laughter amongst the French subsided and uncomfortable glances were cast in the direction of the Velucci.

It was Bianca who took charge, motioning to the guests with a forced smile and Valentina felt her hand taken and placed on her husband's arm to lead the way from the chapel to the main hall of the Palazzo where the wedding banquet was to take place.

Once they were all seated, with the bride and groom in the places of honour, and the wine began to flow, everyone slowly relaxed. The thought of the pile of ducats which it had been agreed should be his, guaranteed Guido's congeniality towards Valentina who could scarcely take in what was happening. The day's events had kaleidoscoped into the mass of whirling colour which was her wedding feast as the company danced and laughed and the wine flowed in full measure. The heavy gold ring on her finger was far too big for her and she felt she could hardly lift her hand for its weight as it slipped around when she reached for her cup.

Her husband, the enigmatic stranger who sat beside her, leaned across and his warm breath fanned her ear as he whispered, sending shivers of a vague excitement down her spine.

"My apologies for the lack of a proper wedding ring Madame, but as you know we had to make do with what was to hand in our haste."

She felt his glance on the garish yellow dress and fought down her mortification at the obvious meaning behind his words, then as she drew breath to reply he continued in that husky voice, "Be assured, Valentina, that any wife of Raoul de

Baisleon will have access to the finest of materials and the most skilled of dressmakers as well as some of the rarest jewels in either France or any of the city states."

Somehow his boasting made him seem younger and her fear and shame receded a little. His use of her name made her pulses jerk and for the first time his own name registered in her mind – Raoul – she would not dare to use it. She could not imagine herself on such easy terms of intimacy with the dangerous male at her side, for she was sure he was dangerous although she could not have said why.

Keeping her voice calm and polite she answered, "You are most kind Signore. You may assure yourself that I shall not bring shame on you for my dress and..."

He cut her short with a growl. "What is mine is yours. I am quite sure that you will not shame me."

She looked straight into his eyes and for a second it seemed as if they were alone. Then she whispered, "Thank you...Raoul." There! She had said it. His smile was fascinating and it was only with an effort that she looked away to answer a question from one of the Frenchmen at her side.

Slowly Valentina relaxed and started to enjoy the festivities. Her conversation became much more lively and spontaneous and in spite of her garish, ill-fitting outfit and her badly dressed hair, she soon had the French captains hanging on her words as she gestured and laughed and charmed them into delight. Her lord watched her from beneath hooded lids, keeping his thoughts hidden and talking little, only noting the becoming flush in his wife's cheeks and the gleam of light on her raven tresses. His eyes lingered on a glimpse of high rounded bosom as she leaned forward to reply to a remark from one of his compatriots, the overlarge neckline of her dress not contributing to her modesty.

As the evening wore on, Valentina found her head spinning a little and her tongue lacking control as the unaccustomed strength of the wine entered her blood. She was tinglingly aware of the man at her side who was now her husband and she slanted many a considering glance beneath her lashes, noting the long slender fingers which she knew held a hidden strength and the powerful thighs which brushed her own as he stretched his long legs beneath the table. Her heart contracted as he caught her look and a lazy smile curved his mouth, his eyes sliding caressingly down her body.

Suddenly the way she was dressed did not matter. She felt as though he saw beneath the ugly clothes to the slender curves of her virgin's body and her lip trembled, her teeth clenched to control the surge of anticipation which his sensuous regard aroused in her.

Abruptly the Lord de Baisleon put down his cup and rose to his feet, pushing back his chair then he turned to Valentina, and held out his hand without a word. For a moment she hesitated, then as his brows raised at her uncertainty she placed her fingers in his, almost as though grasping at a lifeline. Once more she felt his grip tighten reassuringly as it had at the wedding ceremony and into the silence which had fallen when her lord had risen to his feet, Raoul spoke the words which forestalled the ladies of the Velucci in their movement to escort the bride to bed.

"If you will forgive us Madame Bianca, we shall retire to bed without the aid of the ladies of the household. I am sure that I can provide my wife with whatever she may need in the way of a maidservant and we are sure that you would prefer to continue with the delightful festivities you have provided."

There were gasps and a few ribald comments, and Valentina saw her mother's lips tighten and Medina flounce sulkily back into her chair as she saw a chance to spitefully frighten her younger sister foiled by the French lord.

On trembling limbs Valentina walked close to her husband as they left the hall, the voices rising once more behind them in speculation and laughter.

Through the cool quiet passageways they walked, Raoul shortening his stride so that his wife could keep pace with him. The damned yellow dress seemed to keep tripping her up and his arm went about her shoulders to support her and then to turn her as they reached the door of his chamber. Once inside her eyes took in the great canopied bed and his belongings flung carelessly over the chairs then panic clutched at her throat and she turned to fly, only to be met by the solid wall of green velvet which was her husband's chest as he stood silently behind her.

She raised her eyes to his beseechingly but his gaze held only desire and as she made a movement to evade him his hands came up and strong fingers bit into her shoulders to hold her still.

"What Madame? Do you seek to leave me so soon after our wedding? I have long been aware of the inconsistency of women but I did not think that you would be so eager to return to the loving bosom of your family."

His words drained all the will to flee from her body. He was right. Where could she go? She was committed to him for good or ill and it was his right to do with her as he pleased. She shuddered and a small frown of concern puckered Raoul's brow. Still keeping his hold upon her he led her across to a small table which held the customary flagon of wine and poured some of the red liquid into a cup, holding it for her to drink as though she were a child, then his fingers slid from her shoulders pushing down the sleeves of the overlarge dress to reveal the smooth flesh beneath.

With a cry she tore herself from his grasp and fled across the room to the door only to find him there before her. She stumbled against him and was caught up in his arms to be carried to the bed. She fell back into the soft cushions and before she could rise, his weight had pinned her beneath him and his fingers grasped the back of her head to hold her mouth against his in a kiss which demanded surrender and set her thighs aching with desire.

All thoughts of resistance fled against the onslaught of experienced hands and mouth and delicately seeking fingertips. The yellow silk gown was ripped apart with a terrifying ease to be crushed, forgotten, beneath them and when he raised himself from her to remove his own clothes she cried out at the terrible sense of loss which assailed her. Then he was back again, murmuring her name over and over in his husky voice, soothing the brief agony of her deflowering with tender lips and cradling arms.

Raoul de Baisleon was accustomed to the very experienced ladies of the French court. Confronted with the soft virginal innocence of his young wife he found his warrior's heart stirred by emotions which were totally foreign to him. He tried to be tender, to go softly with her but as his mouth roved the sweet soft skin of her cheek, then her throat and finally the delicate swell of her breast, his heart beat an erratic echo to the chaos of passion and desire warring within him.

Impossible to be gentle when blazing need fired his blood, yet when it was over he rubbed his forehead against hers, his breath coming unevenly as he held her close and kissed the tear stains from her cheeks. "Forgive me if I hurt you." He whispered, then not knowing what else to say he pillowed her head on his shoulder and closed his eyes, with no further word sliding into sleep. Valentina was wakeful for a time, staring into darkness and attempting to sort the chaos of her emotions before exhaustion overtook her and she too slept, enfolded in the arms of the French captain.

CHAPTER III

When Valentina awoke in the morning, he had already left her. For several minutes she hovered between sleep and wakefulness, her mind exploring the various aches and rawness new to her body, almost savouring them in a strange sort of way. She was glad that she was alone for she was not sure she could face him just yet. Not until she had recalled fully all the events of the previous night, the moments of hurt as well as tenderness and passion.

A soft tap at the door forced her into the day and when she gave the command to enter, it was the face of a boy, a boy she did not know, which poked around the door. They stared at each other for a moment then, "Louis, Madame." He introduced himself. Satisfied that she was decently covered, he came into the room carrying a bowl of hot water, cloths for washing and drying and from his belt with a triumphant flourish after placing his burden on the table, two small vials of what turned out to be perfume.

"Food, Madame. Two moments." He mimed eating, making her smile then he was gone, leaving Valentina to ease herself from the bed.

The hot water was a blessing to which Valentina was unaccustomed and she savoured the comfort of it as she washed, tenderly bathing those parts which still stung her and the bruises now appearing where Raoul had been a little rough. When finally she was ready to dress, she stared at the crumpled ruins of the yellow gown. Hopeless to even try and mend it.

Louis' knock made Valentina leap to the bed, wrapping the coverlet about her once more before giving permission to enter. As the boy fussed about, clearing away the water and used linen and setting her food where she could reach it, the pantomime of asking for clothing began. Eventually the message was understood and the boy who, it seemed, was her husband's page, left to find wearable clothes for his mistress. As Valentina settled down to eat, the main thought in her mind was that she should start learning something of her Signor's language. She felt poised on the edge of life, not knowing what lay before her yet exhilarated and eager to discover whatever the future might hold.

The arrival, sudden and bustling, of her mother Madonna Bianca Velucci in full sail, startled Valentina back to the present. One sweeping, knowing glance took in the remains of the yellow gown, the state of the bed sheets and her daughter's flushed cheeks then stifling a relieved sigh, Bianca motioned to the maids following behind her. Their arms piled high with fresh linen, it did not take them long to restore the room to order.

"All went well ?" The question was quiet but also anxious and on an impulse Valentina touched her mother's hand.

"He is no monster, Mama. Yet he is a man who must have his way. He does not make me fear him, though, and I think the match is good for me."

The relationship between Bianca Velucci and her daughters had never been demonstrably affectionate. Each time her pregnancy had produced another female instead of the much-desired heir, Bianca had felt her husband's disappointment and anger. However, a fierce surge of protective mother love now made her grasp her youngest daughter to her breast and brought an unaccustomed tear to her eye.

"You will be going far away. The French king moves on Naples and even though his army is strong there will be dangers for you. Watch also for jealousy at the French court for it is clear that your husband, although so young, is powerful and well thought of by his king. There will be many sour faces at this marriage I think."

"Have no fear for me. You know I am not one to be easily bullied or deceived."

That brought a smile to Bianca's lips. Thinking of the rages her husband had flown into over Valentina's tricks in the past she was almost inclined to feel pity for the Frenchman. Still she gave a last warning.

"Your husband has ultimate power over you. Try and be sensible. Do not annoy him beyond his tolerance. Now ! Enough of warnings. There is no time to provide you with new clothes but we have done our best so that you will not seem a pauper amongst the French. I can spare you Deodora as maid for the price the Frenchman paid for you was high."

The sudden return of Louis caused a minor diversion but Bianca put him to good use helping to sort through the gowns and other items donated to Valentina's wardrobe by her sisters.

There was one of those moments, then, when everything seemed to stand still. The maids, for the most part, had finished their tasks and left. Valentina had finished eating and was dressed. The room was tidy and quiet.

Into that moment stepped Raoul de Baisleon.

Valentina's heart almost stopped beating. It seemed as though they were alone in that room and her body was recalling every touch of his lips, every brush of his fingers.

"Madame." Just the one word but somehow she knew that he too was thinking of those things.

Bianca Velucci watched with great satisfaction. Although her marriage to Guido Velucci was not one of love nor passion, yet when she was young, there had been a taste of such a thing as this which she now sensed between her daughter and the Frenchman.

"Has Louis been of help to you, Madame? Do you have everything you need ? We shall be staying longer than I originally thought so you have some time yet with your family, another week or so I think. However when we do go you must be ready."

Bianca ventured a reply. She was not entirely

sure of him. "We have tried Monsignor, in what little time we have had but in spite of your generosity, my resources are few."

Those piercing amber eyes smiled at her. "Do not worry Madame. As soon as possible I shall make sure that my wife lacks for nothing. Now." He turned to Valentina. "The king wishes to meet you so if you feel you can face the French court, we are to present ourselves at the Medici palace this afternoon."

"I am ready at any time to go with you Monsignor." Valentina stood straight and held his gaze without flinching so that briefly he frowned then the smile was back and he was issuing rapid orders to Louis.

The streets of Florence, which should have been so familiar to Valentina, seemed oddly foreign. French soldiery mingled a little uneasily with Florentine folk, yet they were on their best behaviour under strict orders from their king and his captains. The Florentines were out in force taking advantage of the free spending inclinations of the army so suddenly within their walls.

Raoul de Baisleon's standards were quickly recognised by the French and a respectful path cleared for them. There were a few cheers and whistles at the sight of the woman, clearly of quality, riding next to the Lion of France and enjoying all the attention as they made their way through the throngs with difficulty to finally reach the palace built by the Medici.

Once past the heavy guard at the gates, servants moved quickly to hold their horses and attend to their needs and Valentina found herself being introduced to a most handsome young man who bowed before her with a flourish and took her hand to kiss.

"My lieutenant of lancemen, Madame, Alain d'Imoges. My valued right hand and my very good friend."

Twinkling blue eyes were a shock beneath a mop of dark hair and Valentina was impressed by the charm of his smile.

"Enchanted, Madame. I can understand now why Monseigneur was so suddenly and deeply smitten. I must apologise for my absence from the wedding celebrations but it was unfortunately my turn as guard commander for the king."

"You are forgiven Monsignor..."

"Not Monsignor, Madame, merely lieutenant..."

"Oh ! Well, you are forgiven in any case..."

"I hate to interrupt but the king awaits."

Valentina and Alain d'Imoges looked up a little guiltily at the Lord de Baisleon for his voice did hold a touch of cold impatience, then Valentina put her hand into that of her husband and stepped forward to enter the old palace of the Medici and meet her king.

Charles was so distressingly ugly that Valentina was shocked. His head was very large in proportion to his body and his limbs seemed to jerk disjointedly. His lips were large and loose and wet and Valentina fought down a whisper of revulsion. However, he was very charming although she found it difficult to understand what he said.

"Well now, my Lion, I see why you have decided to settle down and leave such a trail of broken hearts languishing in your wake."

Something faintly malicious in the tone of Charles' voice made Valentina more alert to what he was saying. Also she could sense a little discomfort on the part of her husband as he shifted uneasily next to her.

"You do realise, Madame, that you have put more than one pretty nose out of joint in landing this prize – this so far unattainable prize – of the Lion of France ?"

Valentina decided that her best course of action

was to pretend to be stupid, so she smiled prettily and merely answered. "Yes Sire."

Charles blinked and tried again.

"Oh yes. There will be many a young maid — and not so young — and not even so much a maid — who will have the daggers out for you my dear. So watch your back and beware the dangers of taking such an eligible and normally such an obliging man, off the market. That is unless you intend to continue to oblige the ladies..?" He grinned at Raoul like a shark.

Valentina was stunned. Surely this ugly oaf of a man could not be saying what she thought he was saying ? That not only had her husband been one to indulge in affairs with all and sundry, but that he may have every intention of continuing to do so ?

Raoul de Baisleon was furious with his king. He was long familiar with Charles' predilection for causing trouble and stirring up gossip, but that he should so blatantly try and upset Valentina at their first meeting, appalled him. He glanced at the young girl standing next to him and was amazed to see her smiling.

"Yes Sire. Thank you Sire." Behind that facade of blank smiling stupidity, Valentina's mind was seething. She would simply pretend that she had not really understood what had been said, but she certainly intended to find out exactly what this was all about, in her own good time. Raoul was relieved. Valentina had not understood the king's loose, lisping words. Time to withdraw.

"If you will excuse us now, Sire. I shall return my wife to her family so that she may spend what short time we are here in Florence with them."

"Certainly, certainly. Let her enjoy the security of their love while she may. Before she is cast to the wolves. Or should I say wolverines?" Charles laughed like mad at some private joke and Raoul ushered Valentina quickly out of the room. When they had left, Charles sat back with a loose smile on his face. He was not sure of the girl. He knew he had angered Raoul — but the girl ? Was she as stupid as she seemed ? Ah well. Time would tell. Serve de Baisleon right for going ahead and marrying without consulting him — and he knew a certain French lady who would not be too happy about all this either.

Alain d'Imoges was still waiting where Valentina and Raoul had left him.

"A week, at least, before we can get out of here, Alain. Escort Madame back to her father's house then return here to me. The king holds council tonight and I want to be in possession of every scrap of information you have on the Pope and his forces. Especially the whereabouts of his commander..." Raoul glanced down at his wife and cut short whatever it was he had been about to say.

Valentina was silent. Two days ago she had been just the youngest daughter of Guido Velucci, very low down the scale of importance in Florentine society. Now suddenly this man, this foreigner, for whatever his reasons, had marked her for his own and she found herself already becoming involved in the plotting and scheming of the French court. She glanced up to find him watching her with that expression in his eyes which made her recall with a shivering yearning all that had passed between them the night before.

"Madame, Alain will take you home." He hesitated a moment and his voice was soft. "I shall not see you tonight, but if you need me, Alain will find me."

He was close, so close and his breath was warm. Valentina tilted back her head.

An explosion of sound, shrill and invasive jolted them apart and Valentina felt herself tense inexplicably as a group of women erupted into the courtyard. They were chattering like magpies and squealing with laughter and as soon as their leader spotted Raoul de Baisleon and his wife standing there, she headed straight for them.

"My Lord de Baisleon, you are the most wicked man. To marry in such haste – and so secretly. It makes us wonder – why?" Her voice lifted and she glanced at Valentina with her plucked eyebrows raised and her eyes raking the younger girl from top to toe with a disdain so obvious that even her cronies had the grace to be embarrassed.

For the first time in her life Valentina was at a loss. This creature before her was so impeccably groomed, dressed in the height of French fashion and blazing with jewels, her lips reddened, her skin so white. And her manner towards Raoul de Baisleon, although she did not touch him and Valentina had not understood much of what she had said, was so provocative, so possessive, that it was obvious now exactly why the French king had been so disbelieving at the marriage of the Lion of France to such an insignificant person as Valentina Velucci.

Valentina placed her hand upon her husband's arm.

"Monsignor. Will you not introduce me to your – friend?"

Raoul was cursing his bad luck at this encounter with the woman who, up until three nights ago, had been his regular bed-mate. His smile was strained.

"Certainly. Madame de Brieur, wife to one of our most eminent captains. Madame, my wife the Madame Valentina de Baisleon."

The combination of the sound of her new name, plus her instant dislike of the woman before her, bolstered up Valentina's confidence.

"Delighted, Madame. It will be so comforting for me when we leave Florence to know that there is an older woman at court whom I know already, so that not everyone will be a stranger."

A choked laugh from Alain d'Imoges was hastily turned into a cough and as Valentina smiled sweetly at Madame de Brieur, Raoul translated her words as carefully as he could.

Camille de Brieur was a dangerous woman. She did not intend to lose such a rich and powerful lover as Raoul de Baisleon to some foreign chit of a girl but she knew that now was not the time. But her time would come. No doubt about it.

"My dear, I shall be glad to help you in any way I can. And take no notice of any stories you may hear about this man of yours. Court gossip, my dear, court gossip." Then she was gone, with her sycophants about her, fluttering, laughing, casting speculative glances at the new young wife of the Lion.

Valentina did not bother to ask for a translation of Camille's parting shot. She brushed briskly at her dress.

"Well now, Lieutenant d'Imoges..."

Her pronunciation of his name made the young man smile.

"Let us go. My mother and sisters will be burning to hear all about my meeting with the king and these other – people."

Raoul de Baisleon was left standing, watching them as they left. His expression was closed. For one who had held such power as he since an early age, it was easy to mask his thoughts and feelings.

Not so Valentina. Alain d'Imoges glanced uneasily at her as she urged her horse forward through the crowds, heading back towards her home as though the devil was at her heels.

When they reached the Palazzo Velucci, Valentina was so distressed that she could barely thank the lieutenant for his care of her before she fled to her room, praying for solitude, hoping that neither her mother nor any of her sisters would waylay her. As the door closed tight behind her, she leaned back against it thankfully, struggling to calm herself.

That slut ! A married woman who was obviously expecting her illicit liaison to continue. Indeed it seemed the whole court was expecting that marriage would make not one ounce of difference to the appetites of de Baisleon and his mistress. And what of the husband ? Was he so complacent ? Did he not know what was going on? Surely he could not be such a fool. Valentina could hardly wait to meet him.

The burning question for Valentina now was what to do about the situation ?

Shedding her cloak and shoes she climbed onto the bed and started to consider that question. Chewing her thumb she looked at her options. To ignore what had happened and try to keep her husband interested only in her ? To bring the matter into the open and try to wring a promise of faithfulness from him ? To kill Madonna de Brieur? Valentina smiled nastily at the thought, then discarded it reluctantly. Her main problem was that she had not known her husband long enough, did not know him well enough to decide what the best course would be. Best, perhaps, to continue to pretend ignorance and play the cards as they fell.

Valentina sighed. That was the thing to do she supposed.

Restored to her usual brisk self-confidence she started to ferret through the boxes of belongings which her mother had brought her that morning. Everything had been neatly sponged and pressed and she was so grateful for her sisters' generosity but an image of that woman, that sophisticated, scintillating bitch, kept intruding into her mind and spoiling her pleasure in the gifts.

The rap at her door was a welcome interruption. "Your lieutenant, Valentina, wishes to speak with you." Bianca Velucci was on her guard, suspicious of such a handsome young man in close proximity to her daughter. She stood reluctantly to one side to allow the young man to enter. Alain d'Imoges was apologetic. "Forgive me, Madame. Monseigneur charged me with a small task and we left so quickly that it slipped my mind."

"Yes, lieutenant ?" Valentina was curious. The young man seemed pleased, almost triumphant over something.

"I was instructed to give you this for your personal use, Madame. Buy whatever you need, Monseigneur said. Just let me know if you require more."

The weight of the money bag which he handed to her had Valentina gasping and even her mother's eyes were bulging at the French lord's generosity to his wife. "Thank you, lieutenant."

He grinned, enjoying their amazement. "Do not forget, Madame. If you need more you have only to ask."

"Yes. Certainly. I will." She could hardly utter the words.

When he had gone, mother and daughter took the bag over to the bed and reverently opened the strings. For a moment Valentina stood, her hands hanging loosely at her sides, then she took the bag and tipped it upside down, spilling the gleaming contents onto the bed-cover.

"Sweet Infant Jesus !" Her mother gasped and pressed her hands to her mouth.

The stream of ducats seemed never-ending and by the time the last gold coin clinked onto the pile, Valentina was trembling.

Bianca cast her arm about her daughter's shoulders and gave her a hug. "Steady, daughter. It seems you are most fortunate in your Signor. Just be glad. Now! I shall send for the dressmakers and you can make an old woman very happy by allowing this mother to dress her daughter as she would have wished had fortune been kinder."

There was a little difficulty at first with finding a tailor prepared to attend upon them. Guido Velucci had reneged on so many debts. Eventually a sight of the bag of ducats was so persuasive and thus began a whirl of measuring, twirling, cutting, snipping and stitching at the end of which Valentina remembered she had eaten nothing since the morning.

Louis was sent to fetch sustenance from the kitchens and Valentina tucked in hungrily, watching her mother and her sisters, who had not taken long to appear on the scene, hot on the heels of the dressmakers, exclaiming and squabbling over lengths of material and trimmings.

"Don't do that !" Her sharp order silenced them, all eyes turning to stare at her. "There is no need. He has given me enough to outfit an army. Enough for all of us."

The silence lasted a few seconds before the eruption of jubilation, of celebration, could be heard in the alleyways below the Palazzo.

The dark shadow which moved there glanced up, pausing momentarily to listen before slipping away to join his three henchmen waiting with the horses.

The four horsemen, Piero del Aguila in the lead,

then disappeared into the night, heading south to Rome. Cesare Borgia, commander of the Papal forces awaited, eager for news of the French and anticipating the large sum of money carried by del Aguila, payment with interest of Guido Velucci's debt. The money which had purchased a wife for Raoul de Baisleon, the Lion of France.

CHAPTER IV

Valentina had not seen her husband for a week.

At first she was not too bothered because she had heard him talk of the council with the king. But when three nights had gone by without sight nor sound of him, even her sisters were glancing at her with pity.

Slowly her fury built.

He was with the woman de Brieur. He had to be. She tried to question Alain d'Imoges.

"These councils of your king? Do they always last such a long time?"

"Sometimes." The young man was sympathetic but still on his guard. "When the king is obsessed with an idea then everyone must dance attendance on him."

"Even the women?" Valentina threw the question

at him, glancing quickly over her shoulder to catch his reaction.

Spreading his hands d'Imoges shook his head. "Madame, please. There is no need for this. Whatever Monseigneur may have done in the past, he is not one to sully his own marriage vows."

"If he has been prepared to sully those of a fellow captain, then why not his own? It is not as if he loved me, not as if I brought him riches or powerful alliances. He owes me nothing. He does not even need to worry about offending my family because all he would have to do would be to offer my father more money!"

With the words she took a fistful of the gold which was lying on the table by her bed and hurled it across the room.

D'Imoges winced and tried again to calm her. "Think, Madame. Why would he part with so much money for someone of so little importance? I mean – he did not need to offer marriage... " He was making matters worse but he did not know how to stop, how to put things right.

Valentina suddenly wanted to be alone.

"Thank you, lieutenant. I do not need you any more."

Alain d'Imoges sighed helplessly, watching her

shuddering back. What his Seigneur was up to he did not know, but whatever it was it should not be affecting this young girl so.

"Very well, Madame." Reluctantly he left her alone.

It took Valentina a long time to calm down. But calm down she did. The new clothes for Valentina and her mother and sisters had started arriving and the diversion was more than welcome. Determinedly Valentina put on a brave face before her family. Her father had been decidedly put out at the finery which adorned his womenfolk, but as Valentina was now none of his concern he could do very little about it. He decided, therefore, to pretend to his friends that it was he who had been the one to pay for it all.

At least he had paid off that shark, del Aguila, although he now had very little left of the money he had been paid for Valentina. The amount of the interest alone had staggered him. He pushed away the resentment and concentrated on the moment at hand.

He had to admit that his youngest daughter looked magnificent in her new finery, though she still lacked any decent jewellery, and even Medina looked better for the dressing up.

At the dinner table that evening he forced himself to remember her name.

"Valentina. It seems I made a good choice in your husband, foreigner as he is." He flashed a smile that was supposed to be affectionate.

Valentina suddenly found it difficult to keep a straight face. She had a good idea what her father was after.

"Yes father. I thank you for such careful consideration."

She could not look him in the eye.

"Ahem! Yes. Well it is a father's duty to look after his daughter's welfare." He risked a glance but was unable to see her expression.

"You are also a dutiful daughter."

She did not reply.

"You have been most generous to your mother and sisters."

Again no reply and Guido was encouraged by her seeming docility.

"Perhaps your father could hope to share in that generosity. After all it is due to me that you find yourself married to so rich a Signor – and young and handsome too. Any girl would be ecstatic at her good fortune."

At that point she looked up at him. He really was

rather pathetic. A bit of a bully, a coward as most bullies are. He was weak and not overly intelligent – but yet he was still her father.

"What happened to my bride price, father?"

Guido blinked and then frowned. He was about to snarl that it was none of her business what he had done with the money, but those steadfast dark eyes, so like her mother's, made him think again. He hated having to answer.

"A particularly dangerous creditor, my dear daughter. A very large debt."

"Is there any left?"

Guido shrugged. "A little." He avoided her gaze, wishing that he had never started this conversation, wishing that he had never got involved with del Aguila and his master, wishing that he had not been such a fool.

"How much do you want?"

"What?" Guido stared at his daughter, scarcely able to believe it had been so easy. He had thought she would make him grovel a little more. After all, he admitted to himself, he had not exactly been a loving father.

"How much do you want? My husband's lieutenant said that I had but to ask."

Spreading his hands, her father shook his head.

"I do not know. That is... I leave it to you."

Even as the words left his mouth he was berating himself for not naming an astronomical sum.

"Very well." His daughter became brisk and businesslike. "I shall provide generous dowries for my sisters, although I had hoped my bride price would do this. I should have known better." Guido coughed, pretending not to have heard that remark. "I shall send my mother an income through the Florentine bankers. For you, a single sum. I shall have to see what Monsignor will allow but I shall ask for as much as I dare."

Stunned, hardly able to stammer his thanks, Guido signalled for more wine and proceeded to toast his daughter, and her French lord in his absence, until far into the night.

Valentina did not stay to hear his compliments. Retiring to her room escorted by Lieutenant d'Imoges, she felt drained, exhausted by all that had happened over this last week, not least by her husband's failure to arrive back at the Palazzo Velucci. He had obviously found more congenial company at the Palazzo Medici along with the other lords who had been billeted in Valentina's home. It was a slight consolation that at least he was not the only Frenchman missing from their host's table.

She stopped at the door to her chamber and turned to look up at the young man who escorted her. "Lieutenant? Tell me... If I was your bride would you leave me so alone?"

The appeal in her dark eyes was such as to make the young Frenchman catch his breath and remind himself vigorously that this was his Seigneur's wife. She was so beautiful that he could not understand how the Lion could bear to be away from her even for a moment. He tried to reassure her.

"Madame, you must understand Monseigneur's position at court. The king often keeps his commanders at his side without thought or consideration and I am sure... very sure, that if it were at all possible he would be here with you. He would be mad not to prefer your company to... to any other."

They both knew who that 'other company' was and Alain d'Imoges fought away that overwhelming impulse to console Valentina with more than just words.

With a wry, sad smile and a sigh Valentina turned away. "Goodnight Lieutenant."

"Sleep well, Madame."

When the door had closed behind her, Alain took a deep breath then slammed his fist at the door jamb before turning away to seek his own quarters.

Valentina felt as though she would never sleep again. Tossing and turning she called herself all kinds of a fool for wanting him, yet want him she did, desperately. Every fibre of her being yearned for him and she was totally bewildered by the desperate hunger which consumed her. Sleep took her by surprise. She did not even realise it had actually claimed her until she was awoken by a stumbling crash and a curse in the dark of the night.

Alarmed, she sat up, clutching the bed covers to her chin and about to scream for assistance until she realised that the clumsy, groping figure looming over her was that of her husband.

"Monsignor!" The wave of joy and anticipation which coursed through her was frightening in its intensity yet as, slowly, the realisation dawned on her that he was drunk she felt that joy replaced by anger. The past days of wondering, of humiliation, of rejection suddenly formed into a hard ball of rage which made her want to hit out at the man who stood over her.

"Get away! Do not touch me! Go back to your whore, foreigner, and leave me alone!" She slapped at his hands as he reached for her.

At first he laughed at her. He was not one who usually allowed the drink to take control, but Charles had been particularly infuriating these last few days and the only way to avoid an argument was to get drunk. Now he had escaped from the pressure and pride to seek consolation with his sweet new wife.

But somehow he thought he must be in the wrong room. This snarling, raging vixen could not be his Valentina.

"Has her husband returned then? Did you have to scramble out through the window..? No. Do not touch me! Leave me!"

Convinced that she was merely playing a game, Raoul fell atop her, crushing her beneath him, seeking that soft skin with his mouth, breathing in the scent which made his senses swim.

Valentina fought furiously. Her body was screaming out for him yet her mind rejected the thought that he could come straight from that whore and expect his wife to open her arms in welcome.

Raoul was beginning to get angry too. She was being ridiculous now. A little pique that he had been absent was to be admired but this spitting obstinate fury was just not to be born. The thing was, that nothing he did or said would calm her. She was hysterical. Now how was one supposed to deal with an hysterical woman?

He did not mean to hurt her. But she would not stop. Would not listen. Until he slapped her. Full on the side of the face.

There was suddenly nothing but stillness and silence in that room. Only their breathing was loud, his harsh and unsteady. Hers sobbing, unbelieving. Of course she had been hit before. Many times, by her father and sometimes by her mother – beaten for tricks and escapades and even for fighting with her sisters. But this. This was different.

Her head was turned away, forced to one side with that slap and the tears glistened on her lashes and trickled down her cheek. The soft skin where his hand had made contact was purpling and he tried to apologise, to make things right. His head was clearing fast and he was appalled at what he had done.

Valentina was not prepared to listen. Her heart was breaking and all she wanted was to be alone. "Go away. Please." She could hardly breathe the words.

Helplessly he tried again. "Forgive me – Valentina. I did not know what I was doing." He tried to pull her into his arms, to console her but she fought free, slapping away his pleading hands.

"Go. Just go." Brokenly, she commanded him.

Sudden anger drove him to his feet. Anger at her and most of all, anger at himself. He had never hit a woman in his life and for him to hit this woman was unforgivable, he knew that. But she would not listen. Very well, he would say no more. Let her come to him. "If you want me, Madame, you have only to say."

"Never! Get out! I will never want you!"

He did not answer, but left, slamming the door hard behind him.

Valentina was left, crying silently but uncontrollably. "Raoul!" She whimpered his name, but he had gone and the sobs shook her body, her fingers trembling over the marks his blow had left behind. How could he do such a thing? The hurt was nothing – physically, but emotionally she wanted to die. She was willing to bet every ducat left in the bag hidden beneath her bed that he would never hit that woman who coveted him, the woman whose lover he had been, whose lover he probably still was.

Shivering, she sought the pitcher of water at the side of the bed and gently bathed her hot cheek.

Here she was, after having longed for him all week, to have lost her temper and provoked him so when her plan had been to enslave him with her beauty and charm, to tempt him away from that other female. What a fool she was.

What had he said? If you want me, you have to ask. How could she ask? Impossible!

Staring into her mirror she could see the bruise spreading and closed her eyes on a groan. Tomorrow her shame would be on show for everyone to see and she had no-one to blame but herself.

Valentina had never been one to wallow in self-pity so now she tried to calm herself, to consider what she should do next.

Sleep. She needed to sleep. Exhaustion dulled her mind and the throbbing in her face. Everything would look better in the morning after a night's sleep. Slowly she moved back to the bed and rolled carefully over onto her uninjured side. Her lids fluttered closed and she slid gratefully into sleep and forgetfulness.

Raoul de Baisleon had never experienced such turmoil. Women had always been playthings to him and he had never taken them seriously. He had never had to. They had pampered him and spoiled him and taught him all the tricks of sexual gratification. Now he was bewildered. His anger had subsided and he was filled with shame, unable to believe that he had hit her.

The French army was to move out towards Rome early the next day and Alain d'Imoges had been sent back to the Palazzo Medici to ensure that the men who followed the snarling lion's head banner would be ready. Raoul had thought to snatch a few hours with Valentina before the chaos of the departure. Sweet Jesus, she did not even know they were leaving. Well, he could not go back to her now so Louis must be the one to inform her and make sure that she was ready when the ladies of the court departed in the wake of the main army. He would send Alain to escort her with a strong personal guard. She would be safe enough.

He would make his peace with her when they reached Rome. His duties would keep him busy and away from her until then anyway and perhaps she would be in a more forgiving mood.

His horse halted outside the huge gates of the Palazzo Medici and he dismounted, throwing the reins to one of his men with a curt command. Not wishing to go back into that part of the palazzo where he might encounter Charles again, Raoul skirted the main buildings and headed for the quarters which housed his men. They would have to tolerate his presence tonight.

As he rounded a corner he bumped into someone hurrying in the opposite direction. A soft gasp and a fleeting scent of perfume gave the woman away.

"Camille!"

"Oh! Raoul... I was...I was just..." Camille de Brieur laughed nervously. "I was looking for you."

"For me? Why? I thought I had made my position clear to you. I am sorry, but we both knew the rules of the game." Something here did not ring true but Raoul was tired and had other things on his mind than past mistresses, however recently discarded.

Camille pressed close, pulling at his cloak and turning him into the shadow of the wall. "You are cruel, Raoul. You could have been a little more – generous." She was talking to him but her glance slid past him, watching the dark shape of someone melt away into the night, only relaxing when the shadow had gone.

"I think you cannot complain of my lack of generosity Madame." He replied stiffly. He was frowning, trying to look into her face, wanting to avoid any doubt about the future of their relationship.

"No. Well. Perhaps you are right. It would not do to be found here like this. Forgive me. Goodnight Raoul."

Her sudden loss of interest left him thoughtful and suspicious. He knew her well and his gut instinct was that she was up to no good but before he could ask any questions, she had gone and he was left standing, staring after her. He stayed there for a few moments then with a shrug turned away to seek his cold and lonely bed.

CHAPTER V

Valentina sat her horse with her head held high and her back ramrod-straight. It had been impossible to camouflage the bruises on her cheek and so she had laughed them off, saying that she had fallen in the dark. Nobody really believed her but none challenged her excuse.

The French army was leaving Florence with a lot less fanfare than when it had arrived and Valentina waited calmly as Alain d'Imoges checked her guard and made sure that all was secure on the baggage wagons before riding to her side.

"You are ready, Madame?" He was solicitous, sympathetic and fully aware from his Seigneur's mood that early dawn that something had gone badly wrong between these two. He avoided looking at the marks on Valentina's face. Merely to see her so abused aroused such a rage in the young lieutenant that he was tempted to challenge his lord.

"Ready." Just the one word but her set expression and the determined line of her mouth gave the word more meaning.

Her mother and father and sisters stood waving until a turn in the streets took them from sight. Guido hugged what was left of the bag of ducats to his chest gratefully and Bianca smiled at the assurance that dowries would be sent to the banks at the first opportunity.

The French ladies travelled to the rear of the army safely escorted by their own personal guards. Valentina spotted Camille de Brieur instantly, the hairs rising on the back of her neck like the hackles of a dog.

Camille was surrounded, as usual, by her chattering magpie court and she made a great show of staring straight at Valentina and laughing scornfully, before whispering and pointing, whatever she said causing all eyes to goggle at the badly marked face of the Lion's wife.

The tide of colour heated Valentina's face and neck and she muttered curses and threats beneath her breath which a young woman of her breeding should never have known. The humiliation of it all burned her soul and she wondered if it was possible to die of a broken heart. Alain d'Imoges, riding unexpectedly alongside her, thought she spoke to him.

"You need something Madame?"

A smile through clenched teeth was her reply. What she needed he could not provide. She needed to wipe the smile off the face of Camille de Brieur and sooner or later she would find some way of doing just that.

The young man shrugged but cast a wary eye towards Camille and her followers, making a mental note to ensure that his mistress came into as little contact with that one as possible.

Camille was delighted with the signs of conflict between Raoul and Valentina.

"Serves the bitch right." She confided in one of her closest cronies.

"Was he violent with you?" The woman was agog with vicious curiosity.

"Of course not. He was completely wrapped around my finger."

"Then why the sudden wedding?" An irresistible dig.

"To divert suspicion of course. You know how jealous Monseigneur can be." Camille wore a smug expression as she answered and her companion nodded although her brows were raised. Everyone knew how obsessed Etienne de Brieur was with his wife. He would do anything for her. Anything.

The truth was that Camille had been growing a little tired of the liaison with Raoul. It had only been the thrill of playing with such power which had attracted her to him in the first place. However, she was always the one to end an affair. How dare he marry that nobody, embarrassing Camille in front of the court? She knew that there would be many a snigger amongst women who had been the butt of her stinging venom in the past, whose men had been the objects of her desire.

She would make life as miserable as possible for the Florentine bitch. Oh, she would make her so sorry that she had ever crossed Camille de Brieur.

Alain d'Imoges, however, hovered like a guardian angel about Valentina. Just when it seemed that Camille had cornered her or engineered an embarrassing confrontation, the young lieutenant would be there to whisk Valentina away or turn aside a barbed or cruel comment with a joke.

Camille fumed and plotted ceaselessly.

They had been travelling for several days when a young squire took advantage of Alain's absence, as he checked the guard about the Lion's encampment, to approach Valentina.

"Your pardon, Madame. Some of the ladies of the court are riding out for a short way and invite you to join them. My Lady de Lorraine has a hawk to fly and she thought it would distract you from any sadness you may have at leaving your home."

Valentina hesitated as she tried to place the squire's face. She needed Alain's advice on this but knew that he would not be back for a while yet. She assessed the young man before her. He seemed personable enough and she knew that she really should make some effort to find friends amongst the French ladies even if only as allies against Camille's vindictiveness.

With a shrug and a sigh she nodded to the squire.

"One moment and I shall be with you. My thanks to the Lady de Lorraine." At least she knew that the Signor de Lorraine was a good friend of Raoul, so surely she should be safe enough. Nevertheless Valentina searched out a small dagger which Alain had given her shortly after their departure from Florence, his words echoing in her head.

"For your protection, Madame. It will not be expected that you might be armed. It might just give you an advantage over any attacker."

Her maid, Deodora, watched as her mistress took her precautions. "Deodora. Inform the lieutenant that I have ridden out with the Lady de Lorraine and that I should not be gone long."

The little maid curtsied her understanding and watched her mistress leave her tent.

When she mounted her horse to accompany the squire, Valentina felt quite confident that she had taken all measures to ensure her own safety and felt a lift of her spirits as they cantered away.

They left behind the main body of the army, riding up into the hills and Valentina found herself enjoying the quietness away from the bustle and noise of the French forces. She became so occupied with her thoughts that it was some time before she realised that they had ridden for quite a distance and still there was no sign of the party of ladies with whom she was supposed to meet. Pulling her horse to a stop she turned to her companion in puzzlement.

"Is it much further? Surely they would not have ridden on without us.?"

"I think perhaps they may have done, Madame. It took me a little longer than I expected to find you and they were somewhat impatient to be on their way."

Valentina gazed around for a moment and then firmly turned her horse's head back in the direction from which they had come.

"There is no sign of anyone. They must have gone on and we have missed them. It might be better if we returned to camp."

"Just a little further, Madame. I am sure they cannot have been gone long and it would be a shame to miss the fun."

Valentina studied him, still trying to remember which lady he served and not really sure that she liked his expression, which seemed crafty, his eyes avoiding hers as the silence between them lengthened.

"I like this not. I shall return to camp. You may follow if you wish."

To Valentina's dismay, instead of falling in with her wishes, the squire leaned down and caught her horse's bridle near the bit, pulling it roughly to a halt.

"Not so fast, Madame. There are other plans which have been made for you and you do not escape us so easily."

Furious now at her own stupidity, Valentina wrenched on her reins causing her horse to rear up, squealing in pain and almost unseating her. The bridle was torn from the squire's grasp to the accompaniment of some foul cursing from the young man and Valentina laid her whip to her horse's flanks and leaned low over its neck urging it to a gallop, away from her would-be abductor.

Frantically she clung to her mount, hoping that she was going in the direction and calling herself all kinds of a fool for not waiting for Alain. A movement caught out of the corner of her eye alerted her to a line of horsemen who had appeared over the brow of a hill to her left. They thundered down the slope obviously with the intention of cutting her off. She was somehow sure that they were not on her side.

Desperate now and almost sobbing with fear, Valentina changed direction and headed for some trees which she hoped would conceal her from her pursuers.

The squire was close behind her and Valentina was cruel in her use of her whip, terror driving her on until, with a gasp of thankfulness she passed into the cool shade of a small but fairly dense wood.

As she pushed frantically through the thickets, she glanced over her shoulder to see the squire, his face red with fury and exertion, close on her heels, shouting and waving to the small band of horsemen who followed, urging them to hurry.

Suddenly, Valentina's horse veered sharply to the left, throwing her off balance to be swept out of the saddle by a low hanging branch. With a shout of triumph the squire saw her fall and threw himself from his own horse to pinion her to the ground.

She dazedly tried to focus her eyes upon him. His dark hair clung to his forehead with sweat and his lips were tight with contempt.

"You bitch!" he snarled. "'Tis time someone taught you your place."

Through reeling senses Valentina felt all the bitter resentment and frustration which she had been suffering during these past days surge through her body, lending her a strength she did not know she possessed. She screamed with rage as she struggled with her captor, bucking and heaving beneath him. Her fingers brushed against, then grasped with deadly accuracy, the hilt of her dagger, plucking it from the sheath at her belt and raising to strike unerringly at the great vein in her assailant's neck.

For one long moment all movement was stilled as she stared up at him. He opened his mouth to scream but all that came forth was a great jet of blood which soaked Valentina's face and hair and gown as he fell forward.

Gritting her teeth to hold back hysteria, Valentina pushed at the body atop her until it rolled away, freeing her to stumble to her feet as the other horsemen pursuing her closed on the wood.

With no time to catch her horse and flee, the shivering, trembling girl snatched up the dagger once more and scored the flanks of the horses, eliciting a scream of pain followed by a blind, panicking flight by both animals, leaving a crashing trail for all to see.

As the first horseman entered the wood and squinted to adjust his vision to the gloom under the trees, Valentina threw herself on the body of the squire, tumbling both it and herself into the concealment of the thick bushes away from the spot where she had fallen.

Tense almost to screaming point with fear, Valentina closed her eyes to blot out the wide stare of the dead squire at her side then she fought to control her gasping breath as her pursuers halted their horses above her and studied the ground.

"It seems he caught up with her here. There is blood. I hope the young fool has not damaged her."

Valentina's eyes flew open in shock at the words spoken in French. There was only one person who she could think of in the French camp who might want rid of her. Her husband's slut.

Cautiously she lifted her head to see who had spoken but did not recognise any of those who crowded the wood in pursuit.

As she watched, the leader of the group gestured in the direction which the fleeing horses had taken and they all followed the false trail like fools. When the sounds of pursuit had died away, Valentina gave a small sigh and her senses left her.

The two bloody horses which Valentina had used so cruelly did not stop their flight until they reached the French camp, causing a great uproar as they were caught and Valentina's mount was recognised.

It was a white faced Raoul who hauled a sobbing, terrified Deodora to her feet and shook her while he fired terse questions at her.

"When did she leave? Who did she go with? Which direction did they take? Answer me wench, or I'll have your head for complicity in this deed."

He shook her so hard that she almost was insensible before Alain d'Imoges stopped him.

"Monseigneur, you will kill her if you persist in this and then we shall discover nothing."

Taking a deep, controlling breath, Raoul nodded at his lieutenant who cautiously let his arms drop and as his lord simply stood staring ahead with glittering intensity, Alain elicited from Deodora everything she knew.

It was a grim, determined band which set out on the trail of the Lady Valentina and those seeing their expressions crossed themselves and thanked God that they were not the object of the search.

It took them an hour to find the tracks of the horsemen who had pursued Valentina into the trees. The broken branches and trampled grass told their tale and Raoul cursed as he dropped to one knee to examine the bloodstained ground where Valentina had stabbed her attacker then his head flung up at the sound of a movement from the bushes below him.

Drawing his sword, his face as deadly as the lion for which he was named, Raoul approached the concealing branches beneath which Valentina was concealed. The sight of her, bloodstained and ragged, brought panic. He fell forward and snatched her into his arms.

Valentina thought she was dreaming as she was gathered close and gently examined for injuries. She still clutched her dagger in her hand and Raoul carefully prised loose her fingers and took it from her. It was only then that he took notice of the body of the squire lying half-hidden in the leaves.

"Drag him out. Let us see his face."

There was a strange silence as the squire was rolled over and his features came into view and Valentina frowned at her husband's suddenly shuttered expression.

"Bury him! Say nothing of this to anyone."

She was lifted and carried to his horse and then as he cradled her in his embrace she allowed herself to drift away again, deciding to sort out everything later. When her senses returned.

CHAPTER VI

There was a wary alertness about the French army as it approached Rome which was a compliment to the reputation of Cesare Borgia. The man's devious abilities were well known but Charles relied heavily on the knowledge that the inability of the city states to form a strong alliance against him would ensure the French superiority in battle.

Valentina took time to recover from her ordeal at the hands of Camille's squire. Raoul had been most attentive, but politely so. He did not stay long when he came to enquire after her health and she realised with a sigh that all was not mended between them. This in spite of the fact that she knew he had been frantic at her disappearance. Alain had made sure that she knew of the Lion's feelings on that point.

She had waited for Raoul to bring up the subject of the squire she had killed but still he said nothing. So far as Valentina was concerned, there could only be one reason for his silence. He wanted to protect Camille de Brieur.

Camille, herself, also stayed out of Valentina's way, proving to Valentina without a doubt that the Frenchwoman had indeed tried to get rid of her rival.

Truly, it was a deep sense of shame which kept Raoul away from Valentina. He did not expect her to forget the way he had treated her and now he had the added worry of knowing that Camille was not about to be as easily discarded as he had hoped. He should have known that she was up to something that night in Florence, in the Palace of the Medici, when he had caught her abroad in the darkness. What a fool he had been!

Alain d'Imoges was Raoul's trusted confidante.

"Keep her safe. For the moment things are difficult..." Even with Alain, Raoul refused to explain too much. All he could do was rely on Alain's friendship and unquestioning loyalty.

He could see no way of putting things right between Valentina and himself as things stood, for his pride would not let him abase himself and somehow he knew that she would not come to him either. He had to force himself to concentrate on the advance on Rome.

Charles watched the situation with malicious glee, making a point of asking after Madame de Baisleon at every opportunity. When they reached Rome, however, he needed all his wits about him to handle the seething cauldron of suspicion and intrigue that was the Papal Court.

Valentina was exhausted.

The bruises had faded but her resentment grew the longer Raoul stayed away from her. It seemed that he had meant what he said when he had told her that if she wanted him, she would have to beg him to come back to her. Even Camille's plot to get rid of her had seemed to make very little difference to the situation. If anything, it had made things worse, for now she was more certain that her husband wanted to continue his liaison with the French slut.

The vast and echoing dust pile of a palazzo which had been requisitioned as quarters for de Baisleon and his entourage, seemed to epitomise the state of her spirit and Alain d'Imoges was at his wits' end searching for ways to make her smile.

He stood with Valentina and stared around at the

cobwebs which seemed to be all that held the building up.

"It is an insult, Madame, to expect one of such rank as Monseigneur to stay in such a ruin as this."

"Perhaps they wish to insult us. To see how far they can go in their contempt." A true daughter of Florence, Valentina resented the power of Rome.

Alain slid a suddenly mischievous glance at his lady. "If you will excuse me for a while, Madame, I shall see if I can gather some things together to make us more comfortable. If you will choose your rooms I shall send servants to clean and prepare them."

That brought a trace of the smile he was seeking and as her face turned up to his he found himself wondering how on earth his Seigneur could be such a fool as to treat this woman so. He cleared his throat and bowed low over her hand.

"I shall return as soon as I can Madame. Louis will look after you." With that he was gone.

With the little page boy trailing behind her, Valentina walked through the empty rooms, the swish of her gown the only sound, her skirts leaving a trail in the dust. Oddly she felt at home here, perhaps because the Palazzo Velucci had that same air of regretful neglect as this Roman old lady.

The servants of the Lion set about bringing some semblance of order and cleanliness to the old palazzo although little could be done about the state of disrepair.

"Let us hope the roof does not leak." Valentina murmured as they laboured.

Two hours later Alain returned with what seemed to be a treasure house of plunder. He laughed at Valentina's shocked face. "A donation, Madame, from the good citizens of Rome, for your comfort and delight."

"And did these citizens give willingly, I wonder, lieutenant?"

"Ask no questions, Madame."

His grin was infectious and the excitement of unpacking and sorting through the heaps of hangings and plate, candlesticks and even some jewellery cheered Valentina and lifted her out of the low spirits which had plagued her these last days.

Slowly some warmth and beauty was restored to a part of the ageing palazzo and the fires were set to roaring in the kitchens, providing hot water and food for the temporary residents.

Valentina had given up expecting Raoul to come to her, so rather than set a lonely table she ordered her food to be brought to her room, revelling in the cosy intimacy which had been created by Alain's plunder.

Relaxed in the huge chair before the fire, with food in her belly and a sense of deep security enfolding her, Valentina turned her mind back to the problem of her estrangement from Raoul. She had been a fool to lose her temper, she sighed to herself. What man would allow his wife to speak to him so? It was not an unusual thing for men to have mistresses and they expected compliance from their wives. No. She should have used her wits to defeat that French whore – as it was, she had played right into her hands.

The problem was, what should she do now? Could she overcome her pride and beg him to come back to her bed? The very thought of it made her stomach sink. Perhaps she could woo him, enslave him so that he could not resist her. Perhaps... The warmth lulled her into slumber.

It was very late when Raoul de Baisleon found his way back to the palazzo. He had inspected it briefly when it had first been pointed out to him, but even so he was surprised that he seemed to have been deceived by its first appearances. He was very tired. No only had Charles been at his most annoying, sniping at the trouble which Raoul seemed to be having with his wife, but Camille de Brieur had been determined to make things more difficult for him. She had flirted with him in full view of both her husband and the rest of the French court. The situation, in front of the Pope and his retinue, had been highly embarrassing.

The fires had been banked for the night and as with Valentina earlier, the peace of the old place stole over him, easing his aching muscles, unravelling his tired mind. A flagon of wine and goblets stood ready at the end of a long table and this young warrior whom they called the 'Lion of France' stood lonely as he was so used to doing and sipped gratefully at the red wine which warmed his belly.

Inevitably he thought of Valentina and gloom settled heavily on his mind as he considered what a cur he was to have struck her. Her courage when she had been abducted had astounded him and only made his contempt for himself worse. He could not blame her for staying aloof from him.

A footfall made him turn, immediately on his guard, then he relaxed as Alain stepped from the shadows.

"Monseigneur. Do you need something to eat?"

"No. My thanks. I ate with His Holiness and the

king. Although the company was not conducive to good appetite."

"And the Pope's commander, Cesare Borgia, did he make an appearance?"

"No." Raoul shrugged. "He will, no doubt, be up to some mischief and it is as well to be ever watchful with that one." He hesitated a little, then "And Madame, my wife?"

"Exhausted, Monseigneur, but well enough. She ate in her chamber and sent her maid to bed, saying that she would attend to herself. A room next to Madame's has been prepared for you."

There was an uncomfortable silence, Raoul sensing his friend's unspoken condemnation. However, he was not about to explain himself to a lieutenant of lancemen, no matter how close their friendship.

"Lead on."

Alain d'Imoges turned with no further word and his Seigneur followed to the room which had had particular care taken over it by the wife of the Lion. The welcoming warmth enfolded him. He could almost sense her presence, smell her scent, taste her lips and he closed his eyes on a groan. What a mess he had made of things!

"Thank you, Alain. I shall see you in the

morning. Make sure the men get plenty of rest. We'll not be here long I hope and then it's a long haul down to Naples."

"Yes, Monseigneur. Goodnight. Sleep well."

A brief sardonic laugh was the reply and the lieutenant left.

Raoul moved towards the fire, unbuckling his swordbelt and opening his doublet. He ran his fingers through his hair and sprawled into the chair set conveniently there, staring into the low flames glowing in welcome. Pouring more wine into his goblet, he stared into the ruby depths.

He should have known better than to have become involved with Camille de Brieur. He had been warned but in his arrogance he had dismissed those warnings, sure that he could handle her. He had been sure that she was merely amusing herself as indeed was he, but now, not only did she seem determined to hold onto him, but she had turned her vindictive attentions to Valentina. Valentina, so young, so innocent. Easy prey, he thought, for the likes of Camille.

He wondered if Valentina was in bed. Perhaps just to say goodnight. Raoul put down his cup and made his way quietly out of his own room and to Valentina's door before he could think and perhaps change his mind. The door handle was turned and he stepped within.

The fire in Valentina's room was almost out, yet still she slumbered on. Her hair had tumbled into disarray, her gown had slipped from one shoulder and her lashes curled long and dark against her soft cheek. Nothing could have been more desirable to the eyes of Raoul de Baisleon. His stomach tightened and he found his throat had constricted, forcing him to swallow hard. Even as he watched, she muttered and frowned in her sleep and he approached her softly, unwilling to disturb her yet half hoping that she would awaken. She was too deeply asleep and he bent to lift her in his arms and carry her to the bed. A sigh came from deep within and she turned her face into his neck, her breath tickling his skin and sending shivers down his spine.

It was the hardest thing he had ever done in his life, to lay her down, to cover her up and leave her. He did not dare to undress her. That was too much to ask. So the Lion left his wife sleeping and returned to his own room to seek his bed. He determined, however, that he would not let the situation continue. He would apologise. He would grovel. He would do anything to regain her favour and trust and as for Camille de Brieur, she would have to have her position made clearer for he was not prepared to stand for a repeat of this night's little performance.

In the apartments behind the Vatican palace, Cesare Borgia listened carefully to his spy's report. He had not joined in the welcoming banquet for the French king. He had more important things to do .

"The woman has agreed to help us then?"

"For a price, Monsignor."

The Borgia shrugged. "Everyone has a price, my dear Piero. You should know that. And the Lion? I hear he is having problems already with the Velucci girl. Is there a chance, do you think, that she could be recruited?"

"Hard to say Monsignor. She is a beauty. Enough to make you wonder if she is truly of Velucci's loins."

"Hmm." Those eyes, almost black, glittered in the saturnine face of this son of the Pope.

"She is bound to accompany her husband to the feast tomorrow night. I had not intended to go, but I think now that it may be worth my while. What say you?"

Piero del Aguila laughed. "I say, most certainly, Monsignor. It is worth a look – a touch, even."

"Very well. Now. What else is there?"

They consulted long into the night.

Valentina awoke in the early hours and wondered how she had got into bed fully clothed. Shivering, she slid out and undressed to her shift, then jumped quickly back beneath the covers to try and re-discover the dream she had left so reluctantly.

CHAPTER VII

Valentina slept late the next morning. It was the unseasonal sunshine which awoke her, streaming in through the narrow windows and she lay for several moments with her arm across her eyes trying to recall a sensation from the night before. A sensation of a hard mouth brushing her lips so briefly. But that was impossible. It must have been a dream.

Raoul had decided, in view of the tension against the French within the city of Rome, to drill his men on the open area between the old palazzo and the river Tiber. Even when he was satisfied with their efficiency he left a very large company comprising a small force of artillery with the manoeuvrable French cannons and a few score crossbowmen strategically deployed for their protection. Every

French commander took similar precautions. Any man who did not was a fool.

The French lords were bidden to dine with the Pope that evening. Their ladies were also invited.

When Valentina was informed by Louis that she was to accompany her husband, a zip of excitement raced through her.

"You may tell Monsignor that I shall be pleased to go with him, Louis, thank you."

The journey to Rome had been enlivened by lessons in french from Alain d'Imoges and Valentina had been quick to learn. She had no difficulty now in communicating her needs to Louis.

When finally the young page boy came to collect her his eyes widened and his mouth gaped open in admiration. Valentina had taken great and deliberate care over her appearance and the result would be a shock both for her husband and for that slut, Camille, she thought, satisfied with Louis' reaction.

The deep crimson of her gown, shot with silver threads lent a glow to her olive skin and the tight fitting bodice and low cut neckline revealed the stunning perfection of her bosom and the narrow handspan of her waist. The raven tresses had been coiled around her head and confined with a pearl encrusted headdress which seemed a little heavy for her slender neck.

Raoul waited for her in the great hall, talking quietly to Alain and it was only the stunned gaze of that young man slanting over Raoul's shoulder which made the Seigneur de Baisleon turn to see what was the cause of his lieutenant's dumbstruck expression.

Valentina glided close to her Seigneur before drooping slowly before him in a curtsey, her skirts spread out like the falling petals of a scarlet flower.

Raoul cleared his throat yet still his words came hoarsely. "Madame, you are beautiful this evening."

"Thank you, Monsignor." She smiled up into his eyes and he took her hand in that tight reassuring clasp which made her think of her wedding day, and she moved forward at his side, head held high and her heart singing.

The glitter and brightness of the Papal court made Valentina blink as they were announced and made their obeisance before the Holy Father, kissing the ring which he extended gracefully towards them. Roderigo Borgia was a large heavy set man with a hooked nose and a sensuous droop to his eyelids. He put out his tongue and moistened his lips which had suddenly gone dry at the sight of this dutiful daughter of Florence bending before him. Glancing across to his military commander, the Pope was gratified to see his thoughts mirrored on the handsome face of the man who was his son. His gaze returned to the couple before him and as he met the cold menace in the eyes of the French lord who was the husband of this dark flower at his feet, the Pope quickly switched his expression to one of avuncular approval.

At the Holy Father's side Charles' eyes were speculative as he took in the clasped hands of the Lion and his wife. It seemed that she may have forgiven his dalliance with Camille de Brieur – or perhaps had sensibly decided to tolerate the situation. Pity. A little agony amongst his lords made life more interesting. He acknowledged Valentina's curtsey with a smile and an inclination of his head, his eyes following her as she moved away at Raoul's side to their places at the table.

Other eyes than Charles' followed the slim, crimson clad figure.

The Seigneur de Brieur, Camille's husband, was one whose heart held hatred for the Lion of France. He glanced sideways at his own lady to gauge the effect on her of the sight of the Lion now firmly wed, and to a beauty it would be hard to rival.

Camille, aware of her lord's close regard, kept a tight rein on her emotions, only the glitter of her eyes betraying the intense hatred concentrated on the woman at Raoul's side. She had failed once to get rid of the Florentine bitch. She would not fail again.

Cesare Borgia, seated at Camille's left hand, aware of every glance, every murmur amongst the Papal guests, narrowed his gaze in speculation, then leaned forward. "You seem distracted, Madonna. Are you not enjoying yourself? Is there anything I can do?" He smiled charmingly as he spoke and Camille forced herself to answer lightly. She did not deceive the quick malicious mind of this man whose whole life was dedicated to weighing the undercurrents at the Papal court. Undercurrents which had swirled suddenly to life at the appearance of the Lion and his lady.

Unaware of the attention she was attracting, Valentina was enjoying herself. Raoul watched her beneath hooded lids as she chattered and laughed and charmed everyone around her. He nodded a curt permission for her to dance when the first of the many courses had been cleared away. In spite of all his good intentions to apologise to her, he seemed unable to find an opportunity. He would have to wait until later, until they were alone.

As the evening wore on and the wine flowed freely, Valentina found herself growing hotter, and her senses becoming blurred for she was not used to taking so much strong wine. Also, she had to admit that it was not only the wine which was making her head spin. She had acquired quite a following over the evening and the admiration was gratifying in the face of her husband's grim stare. Even Charles led her twice onto the dance floor, something which was noted not only by Raoul but also by those whose business was intrigue and to whom such actions were fuel for scurrilous gossip.

It was quite late and Valentina was starting to feel the onset of an exhaustion caused by the heat and the dancing. It was a little dazedly then that she somehow found herself staring up into a pair of hypnotic brown eyes and she wrinkled her brow in an effort to place the man in whose arms she now danced.

"Ah, Madonna, it grieves me to see that you do not even recall who I am, whereas I could never forget you, nor the flash of your eyes, the flutter of your fingers and the turn of your head." Cesare knew how to turn on his considerable charm. And for a closer look at this woman he was prepared to do anything.

"Forgive me, Monsignor, you are right. I have met so many people this evening and heard so many names that my head fairly reels to remember them all. To be frank I must also admit to drinking rather more wine than is my habit, so you see it is quite understandable if my memory plays me tricks."

This rather disarming confession was met by a rich dark laugh, and the arms about her tightened a little alarmingly before he replied.

"You are most enchanting Madonna. But it seems to me that you are rather flushed. Do you feel ill?"

"No, no, Monsignor, really, it is simply the heat and the dancing. I shall be perfectly alright, thank you."

"Perhaps you would care for some fresh air? There is a quiet balcony close by. Not so far as to be indiscreet, yet far enough to give you a rest from the noise. I assure you that you may depend upon my protection and my discretion."

"Well – I am not sure. I must ask my husband..." A little frantically Valentina searched the tables to find that the place where Raoul had been sitting was empty.

Cesare Borgia watched, amused as she caught

sight of Raoul's head bent close to the blonde coils of a well-endowed young lady who seemed to be entertaining him most adequately. A surge of jealousy ran through her and she turned back to the Borgia with a flounce.

"You are most kind Monsignor. Perhaps just for a few moments."

With a bow and his most charming smile, Cesare offered his arm to the Lady de Baisleon and escorted her from the dance floor and along a short corridor where the sound reached them only as a muffled hum and where the air was much cooler. As they stepped out onto the small balcony Valentina gave a most heartfelt sigh and leaned forward to rest her elbows upon the stone parapet and gaze out over the brightly lit courts of the Vatican Palace.

The Borgia watched her in silence for a short while before stepping close up behind her and placing his hands on her shoulders. She came to herself with a start and a shiver, then realising her position a little belatedly, she tried to move away. The fingers which held her were like steel and she stared up at him, too late recognising the gleam of desire in those velvet brown eyes. "Monsignor, please. You are hurting me."

"I would not wish to hurt you my sweet one.

Come now, surely you do not feel you must act the faithful wife. You must have noticed how engrossed was the Lion? So engrossed that I'll wager he does not even notice you have gone."

As he spoke he bent his head until she could see her own reflection in the depths of his eyes and she froze, mesmerised as his lips took hers in a sudden fierce kiss which sapped her will. Belatedly, she tried to struggle free but he was too strong, too determined to taste the honey of this delicate flower. Then the spell was broken by the familiar husky snarl which constricted her heart.

"You lose your wager Monseigneur. I think you may also lose that which is infinitely more dear to you if you do not move away from my wife – very carefully!"

The threat was all the more dangerous for its very carelessness and Cesare Borgia slowly let loose his hold on Valentina and turned to face his adversary.

"Madame, if you will return to the hall we shall discuss this later."

Valentina stepped close to Raoul, taking breath to explain but he did not even glance at her, never taking his eyes from the tense figure before him, simply repeating, "Madame! If you please!"

Cesare Borgia gave a sneering laugh. "The loving husband! At least I do not have to beat my women to ensure their obedience."

So swiftly that Valentina did not even realise he had moved, Raoul struck, his hand grasping Cesare by the throat in a grip which not even the heavily muscled Borgia could break. For several moments the two men struggled, neither one able to achieve advantage over the other, while Valentina looked on, horrified.

This was all her fault! She should have had more sense than to leave the hall with this man. How had he known that Raoul had hit her? She had said nothing! Desperately she pulled at Raoul's arm. "Please, Monsignor, let him go. He did nothing, nothing! I needed some air that is all. Please, I beg you to let him go."

"She is right my Lion. Let the Borgia go, for I do not wish all my efforts at diplomacy these past days to be destroyed because of a fight over a woman."

The low, barely audible tones of his king acted like a dash of cold water on the French captain, and slowly he forced himself to relax, releasing Cesare Borgia who staggered and clutched at the balcony edge for support. Gingerly he fingered his throat for a moment then with an effort he bowed before

Charles and moved past Raoul to pause briefly in front of Valentina.

"You are generous Madonna. The Lion does not deserve you." His voice was hoarse, his eyes still held that compelling desire. "Should you ever require a favour, I am yours to command." With that the Borgia inclined his head and disappeared along the corridor, away from the feasting.

The three watched him go in silence until Charles spoke in a considering tone. "A strange man. And a dangerous one. You must watch your step until we leave this city my Lion, for it seems to me that this particular Borgia has more than his fair share of power and influence."

"You are right, Sire as always. I shall take great care of myself and my belongings from now on, and if you will forgive us, I feel it is time we left. I am sure my wife is tired."

Charles waved his permission for them to leave and Raoul held out his arm for Valentina. Her fingers were shaking so hard with reaction that she felt sure he noticed but he said nothing and it did not take long to make their farewells to the Pope and gather their escort .

There was no sign of Cesare Borgia.

The return journey to the old palazzo was

completed in silence.

Valentina scarcely dared glance at Raoul. She knew that he stared stonily ahead and she struggled to fight back the tears which threatened to overwhelm her. Why had she been such a fool as to leave the banquet with Cesare Borgia? Sweet Lord, it seemed that she could do nothing right of late. Always in trouble at home, always flying by the skin of her teeth, yet she had never regretted any of her actions so much as she had these last weeks.

Finally they were alone in the dark echoes of the palazzo's hall. The fire still blazed, well fuelled by an attentive servant and Raoul's face was lit by the flickering tongues of flame as he leaned his palms flat against the stone breastwork of the chimney. She could watch him now, staying back a little to allow the shadows to hide her. His shoulders rose and fell on a sigh.

"Well, Madame." An almost incredulous laugh escaped him. "At least Charles seemed entertained by your antics."

"I..." She licked her lips. "I did not mean to cause such trouble. I was hot and dizzy. I needed some air and you..." Her voice strengthened on the memory. "You were otherwise occupied."

Raoul turned, stung, to peer at her through the

darkness. "Do you accuse me, yet again, Madame? Let me remind you that it was not I who was outside, alone on a balcony in the arms of a stranger." His voice was a whiplash and her guilt washed over her. Perhaps she had encouraged Cesare's advances although she had certainly not meant to.

"No. I did not mean that." Flustered, trying desperately to justify herself, her voice was a whisper which he had to strain to hear. "Merely that you were not there for me. What was I to do? He seemed kind...concerned."

"Is a snake kind? Does a viper show concern? Madame, you are sadly lacking in judgement if you can trust such a man as Cesare Borgia." Shaking his head he made a move towards her. Then he stopped short as she backed nervously away.

"Don't do that! I will not hit you again, I swear it."

Valentina stood very still. A yard separated them, yet it may as well have been a mile. He was still angry with her for her foolishness and with himself for losing his head, but when he had seen her in the Borgia's arms... Dear God, how had he not killed the son of a whore?

"You had better go to bed." He turned away,

dismissing her. For a moment she hesitated, tempted to put out her hand, to try and mend the rift between them, but she did not have the courage. She feared the rejection too much. So she left him. Sadly, silently so that almost he did not realise she had gone, then when he did he cursed and sought refuge in the ever available flagon of wine.

CHAPTER VIII

The French forces lingered in Rome until the end of January. By that time the Pope was desperate to be rid of them. Charles toyed with him in his own inimitable way, enjoying seeing him squirm and in spite of all his devious scheming and the frantic comings and goings of his spies, even Cesare Borgia found himself out-manoeuvred.

Valentina saw very little of Raoul. She was not invited again to the Pope's court, or if she was Raoul made no mention of it. The way she felt, she would have refused to go anyway. She was deeply relieved when Alain d'Imoges told her that they were finally leaving.

The weather had continued bright and clear and Valentina's spirits lifted in the hustle and bustle of their departure. The only thing that caused a little dismay was that Alain seemed to be packing almost the entire, supposedly 'borrowed' contents of the palazzo onto their baggage wagons and onto mules which had miraculously appeared from nowhere. When one box fell and burst open revealing its glittering contents she became completely flustered, looking around guiltily, sure that the rightful owners would appear demanding the return of their property. Of course nothing of the kind happened and Alain simply repacked the chest after favouring her with one of his cheeky grins and a conspiratorial wink.

Finally they stretched their great serpentine length out of the hills of Rome towards the south and the rich prize which Charles coveted; the kingdom of Naples. Excitement and anticipation gripped even the ladies of the French court, for everyone, including all the members of the Italian city states themselves, knew that the French were invincible.

Before the first day of travel was over, as the sun was setting in a dark haze of winter beauty, Raoul reined his horse in next to his wife, settling the destrier with a quiet word to match the pace of Valentina's palfrey.

"Is all well with you, Madame? I was too busy

with the king to come and help you."

He looked straight ahead as he spoke and Valentina answered politely although his very presence unnerved her. "Thank you, Monsignor, Alain saw to everything most efficiently." Perhaps too efficiently was the thought which followed, making her smile. He caught that smile and leaned suddenly across to catch the rein of her mount, slowing it down so that their faces were close, those dark gold eyes of his holding her gaze unwaveringly, a kind of desperation in their depths.

"The king has called council again when once we have camped, but tomorrow evening I would wish that we dine together?" Was there pleading in his voice?

Unable to reply because it seemed that all at once she had lost her breath, Valentina merely nodded and, barely satisfied, he let go her rein and cantered forward to join Charles and the other commanders. She watched him until he was out of sight and almost hugged herself with hopeful joy. She knew that it would seem an eternity until the next evening arrived but still – arrive it would.

At the end of the first day's travel from Rome they were camped in the hills. With darkness came a frost and Valentina huddled into her fur-lined cloak, glad of the campfire's leaping flame. The moon sailed full and high, the sky midnight blue rather than black, with the odd luminous trail of cloud lending a wispy magic to the night. Dark shadows of men moved within the circle of the encamped army and the high shrill of a lady's laugh was carried on the cold, still air. One heavily cloaked figure slouched moodily across the edge of Valentina's vision and although it was difficult to recognise who it was, something familiar in the slant of the shoulders, in a gesture, made Valentina frown.

"What is wrong, Madame?" Alain, ever watchful, ever attentive, searched for the reason for her frown.

"Oh! Nothing. I thought... It seemed that I saw... What would Cesare Borgia be doing here, Alain?"

Recognition had come shockingly.

Alain laughed. "'Twas the only way that the Pope could get rid of us, Madame. He styles himself the Pope's Envoy or Legate, yet everyone knows he is a hostage against his father allying himself with Milan and Naples."

Unable to share the lieutenant's amusement, Valentina's murmur held a warning. "Charles does not have his measure. If any man can stop the French, then this son of the Pope is the one."

"Yes, Madame." Alain humoured her. Although Cesare's reputation had reached the ears of the French before they had even entered Italy, still they, for the most part, were so sure of their strength, their superiority, that it was only the Lion of France who was wary of the Borgia.

Unaware of the interest he had aroused by his presence, Cesare was busy cultivating Camille de Brieur. Fascinated and flattered, she almost purred under his practised attentions. Her husband was nervous. His wife demanded so much. The lure of the Borgia bribes, the Borgia gold seemed irresistible.

The French army made good time the next day. The weather continued clear and bright and there was absolutely no opposition to the French advance. The lack of fighting was becoming a bore. Only Raoul de Baisleon kept up the pressure for perfection on his men. When the guard was set at night, it was his men who patrolled the camps, unceasingly vigilant. It was he who chose the camping sites – high ground, easily defended. The Borgia mocked him. "The Lion of France! Who threatens you Monsignor? Or do you tilt at ghosts? You are welcomed everywhere, so why this zeal?"

Raoul shrugged. "Sometimes we have to watch

for the enemy within. You, of all people, should know that. I am not so easily deceived as some."

Cesare hid his gaze, brushing idly at his velvet doublet. What did this captain know? Or what did he suspect? He would bear close watching to find his weakness. Cesare lusted after power – more than anything else he needed to control those around him and it frustrated him that this Frenchman seemed to have no chink at all in his armour. He watched closely as Raoul left the king's tent to return to his own encampment. Perhaps the woman? The wife of the Lion? Cesare smiled in remembered pleasure.

Valentina was flustered to death. As darkness spread its enveloping wings and the campfires were lit she found her stomach cramping with nervous excitement. More than once she needed to relieve herself in the area set aside for her toilette. She had ordered water to be heated for washing but a clumsy servant had overset the pan, putting out the fire. By the time it was re-lit, she was blue with cold from the clear night air and her teeth were chattering, partly from the cold but mainly from nerves. Then it occurred to her that he had not said whether they would dine in his tent or hers and, panic-stricken, she begged Alain to find out.

Alone for the moment after he had left, she twitched at her bodice. Was it too low? Would he think her a slut? Perhaps some wine would calm her? As she poured herself a liberal measure she heard the rustle of cloth at the entrance to her tent and turned to see Raoul himself standing there.

She jumped. The cup fell from her fingers and they both bent at the same time to pick it up.

Fingers touching, crouched low and so close to each other that the mist of their breath mingled, they were caught in a web of magic attraction which took no account of anything that had gone before. Valentina could not look away from him and she was drawn closer and closer, her eyes closing as his lips touched hers. The cup fell again, forgotten this time as Raoul drew her up, not breaking that kiss, but pulling her close into his arms.

She had wanted this moment so much that she thought perhaps her fevered imagination was playing her tricks. Her hands went up to grasp at his hair to pull him nearer and he bent swiftly to lift her and carry her into the back of her tent, to her sleeping quarters. No word was spoken between them. No word was needed.

She need not have spent so much time dressing, for he did not bother with the fastenings of her gown, simply ripping the lace and velvet apart in his eagerness. A brief memory of the destruction of the yellow silk wedding gown made her wonder whether any of her wardrobe would survive his passion until they reached Naples.

Then she dismissed all thoughts of anything except the long sweeping caress of his fingers on her skin. The touch of his lips made her catch her breath as he sought the temptation of breast and flat velvet stomach and surrendering thighs. She bent up one knee at his urging and was really not sure that she should allow him to do the things he was doing. But then, how to stop him? And really she had no desire to stop him. A stray whisper of pity for Camille de Brieur flickered through her mind and was gone.

Raoul was kissing her again, kissing her mouth this time and she placed her palms flat on the muscles of his back, savouring the hardness and ripple of movement there. Then suddenly he was inside her, his flesh invading hers in a sweet burning intrusion which set every nerve a-shiver.

"Valentina. Sweet heart. Forgive me." His broken whispering tore at her heart and she pressed her kisses to his face, to his eyes, his nose, the line of his jaw, his throat, anywhere she could reach, making him laugh briefly before that growing tide of passion swept up and silenced him.

Pleasure rocked his senses in a climax such as he had never, in all his dalliance with women, dreamed could exist. It seemed to go on for ever and then when it was over he was left so weak that a babe could have conquered him.

He sank next to Valentina and caressed her soft cheek with his kiss. She fumbled for the coverlet for the tent was cold and the heat of their love had made them sweat. The dark intimacy of their den was made cosy by the shared body warmth as she wrapped the covers over and above their heads. Raoul cuddled her close against his chest and the steady beat of his heart beneath her cheek lulled her into sleep.

Out in the darkness Alain d'Imoges set the guard. The two within the tent had not eaten and the lieutenant murmured an order to a servant to stoke up the fire which had finally been re-lit and keep some food hot for when they awoke.

As it was, they slept through until dawn. Alain had sought his own sleeping quarters when it became obvious that the Lion and his wife had forgotten about such mundane matters as eating. Only the night guard, therefore, witnessed the sweet parting as Valentina let go, reluctantly, of her lord to allow him to attend to his duties with the king.

She wore nothing under her fur-lined cloak and he gripped the neckline close, holding her prisoner for his kiss.

"I do not want to go." He groaned when finally he lifted his head.

"And I do not want you to go." She whispered back.

"I shall return as soon as I can. As soon as Charles frees me from my obligations."

"Do not forget to eat something. You have had nothing since yesterday morning."

"I have dined on something more delicious than mere food." He grinned at her blush then kissed her again, briefly and hard. "Until later, Madame."

She watched him go, hardly able to believe that things had changed so quickly between them. He had begged her forgiveness for that blow. Begged on his knees in those moments before the dawn, after they had made love again. How could she not forgive him when the sweetness of his kisses still lingered on her mouth?

The guard outside her tent had kept his back determinedly turned towards them as they had made their farewells but now, at her call, he bowed before her. "Madame?"

"Food, Arnaud, if you please? I am starving!"

"Yes, Madame." The burly sergeant smiled and within moments had a bowl of steaming potage ready for her.

She disappeared into the tent and washed and dressed hurriedly while her breakfast cooled. Alain was waiting when eventually she re-emerged into the cold air and the servants started to pack everything onto the wagons ready for moving out.

"A lovely day, Alain." Her skin was glowing and her eyes were alight with the joy of living. Alain thought that he had never seen such a beautiful sight. He lifted her onto her palfrey and mounted his own horse behind her then they moved into their place at the rear of the great army which wound its way slowly southwards.

Raoul cantered back to her often during the day and his attentiveness was carefully noted by those who had an interest in them.

Camille de Brieur fumed and swore to see Valentina dead if it was the last thing she did.

Cesare Borgia considered whether it was to his advantage that the Lion seemed even more enamoured of his lady than ever before.

Charles smiled and wondered what mischief he

could make.

Valentina's happiness was complete and the great invasion of Naples seemed as if it would go ahead without any problem. Until they were stopped by the little town of Monte di San Giovanni.

CHAPTER IX

They had camped where they were for two days. The ladies had been delighted for it meant an opportunity to rest and gossip and air their clothes which had become sadly crushed with being packed for so long.

Valentina had finally made a few friends amongst those who scorned to follow Camille de Brieur. Etoile d'Erpignan was almost Valentina's age and she had shyly introduced herself when it had become obvious that they were not moving any further for a while. She had a small hawk, a present from her husband and she invited Valentina to ride out with her to try the bird for an hour while Charles kept their husbands in close council.

They had fun with the hawk and Valentina was in a happy mood, looking forward to telling Raoul all about it when he came to her tent for the evening meal. He was late and she was starting to worry when finally he came through the open flap.

As soon as she saw him she knew something was terribly wrong. "What is it? What has happened? Is it Charles? What has he done?"

He brushed aside the barrage of questions, his face grim and withdrawn.

"Nothing for you to concern yourself with, Madame." His curt words were hurtful and she drew back confused, not knowing what to do.

Raoul passed his hands over his face and sighed. "I'm sorry. I did not mean to vent my frustration on you."

"Come. Sit down. Eat something and tell me what is wrong."

He allowed himself to be seated and then picked at the food set before him for a time before pushing away his plate and shaking his head.

"'Tis no use. I tried my best but he would not listen."

"Charles? What has he done now?"

"'Tis not what he has done but what he intends to do."

Valentina sat quietly waiting for him to continue.

"The town of Monte di San Giovanni refuses to

bow to him. They refuse to welcome him as he would be welcomed." He brooded for a moment then burst out. "It is not as if the place is of any importance. A tiny little hill town. True, it has walls and could be used in a small way for defence but hardly a gnat's chance of standing against our guns."

"Then what is he going to do?"

He stared at her. "Obliterate it."

She stared back, incredulous. "And you will allow him to do this?"

Raoul jumped to his feet once more, anger in every line of his body. "I do not allow my king to do anything, Madame." His tone softened again. "I tried my best. Anything more and I would have been accused of treason. There are plenty who would rejoice at my downfall and I do not have just myself to think of now."

She was out of her seat in a second and her arms went about him, hugging him to her. He pressed his lips against her hair then put his fingers under her chin to tilt up her face for his kiss. The world swam about her and the thought that he was going to fight tomorrow made her almost desperate in her response, urging him closer, swaying her hips against him.

His breath left his lungs in a groan then he swept her up to carry her to the soft cushions of the bed, falling with her into a maelstrom of whirling desire. His lovemaking was fierce, as though he was afraid he was going to lose her. Clinging to him she returned his caresses wildly, on fire for him, loving the feel of his hard body against her, loving the taste of his mouth, the drugging heat and smell of him. "Raoul, Raoul..." His name, spoken with that faint Florentine inflection became a spur to his passion and Valentina cried out in her pleasure as he lifted her to heaven with him on the wings of his love.

They did not waste the night in sleep. In between their lovemaking they talked. He told her of his home in the southern part of France, describing the warm yellow stone of the great castle which dominated his lands and promising to deck out a solar room for her with the rarest of hangings from foreign parts. He had been left an orphan at merely ten years of age, with a power coveted by many wanting to manipulate the child he had been. He did not trust to anyone so easily these days.

It was well before dawn when Alain came for his lord. She was desperate to keep him with her but could not say so. Instead she made a request.

"Monsignor, please, I would see to your arming before you ride to battle."

The ballads sang of it and although it was no heroic deed he rode away to that day, yet she wanted him to know that, for her, his honour was untarnished, whatever happened.

"I shall return, Madame and you will have your desire." He bowed to kiss her hand then he left with Alain following behind.

By the time the French army was ready, the sun stretched its rosy fingers into the sky. Valentina waited on her husband, taking the heavy swordbelt and fastening it about his waist, sliding his great two-handed sword into the scabbard with difficulty. The helm was almost too much for her and he was forced to help her, his fingers over hers. When he was ready, he beckoned to Bruno, his standard bearer.

"I leave my standard in your care today, Madame, so that it is not sullied by this deed we do." She could hardly bear the agony in his face.

"You may trust your honour in my hands, Monsignor. May God ride with you."

"I doubt He would care to."

The boy, Bruno, came to stand behind her, fighting away the tears. He was very young.

Raoul de Baisleon mounted his destrier and turned away, his face set and, lifting a hand in farewell, cantered to meet his king.

The day went by with mind-numbing slowness as she awaited her lord's return. The din of battle could be heard clearly from the camp and as the hours crept by, the thick black pall of smoke dimming the sky grew longer and more dense.

"Madonna! How long does it take to wipe out one small town and its inhabitants? I thought this army of Charles' was so efficient."

Valentina wrung her hands as she watched the road for the first sight of Raoul. She was offered food but refused it with a shake of her head.

"A cup of wine, perhaps." She told Arnaud, the sergeant who waited on her and he quickly brought her a drink. She cradled the cup in her hands as she still stood at the entrance to her tent, staring at that heavy black mass which hung in the sky. The smell was sickening even from here. She shuddered to think what it must be like at the scene of the battle. Who would have thought that the might of the French army would take even this long to obliterate one small town and its pathetic complement of men?

A sound, a scuffle behind her whirled her about, suddenly on her guard and she tensed in alarm as a figure muffled in a heavy cloak and leading a great grey horse slouched out from behind her tent. Without further thought Valentina hurtled forward, grasping a lance which stood against the wall of the tent and raising it to defend herself against the intruder.

The blow did not descend however, as Valentina stared incredulously into familiar dark eyes which although they mocked her, still held a hint of desperation.

"Monsignor! You!"

"Madonna! You!" Sarcastically he mimicked her but his eyes left her to glance anxiously around before grasping her wrist and pulling her into concealment behind the tent.

"I must get back to Rome. You see what they are doing. They must be stopped and I cannot allow you to prevent me from leaving. You understand?"

She nodded, her mind a whirl of indecision. If she allowed the Borgia to leave she would be betraying her husband, and his king. On the other hand Cesare was right. The French way of making war was horrific, their guns infinitely more terrible than anything this country had ever seen before.

She looked up into Cesare Borgia's eyes, for once uncalculating as he impatiently waited for her decision, then she laid a hand on his breast.

"You must go. You understand I have no desire to endanger my husband by this action and I expect you to consider that fact if it should be necessary at a future date."

Relief flooded his face but he did not turn immediately away. Valentina felt alarm spring anew as he covered her hand with his, preventing her from moving away from him. "Come with me. Sweet Valentina, I can offer you much if you come with me and you would never regret it."

She pushed at him frantically. "Just go. If you are discovered here, now, we are both dead. Go!"

For a moment more he hesitated. "This is not the end of it. We shall meet again, I know it. Until then, Madonna Valentina."

He carried her fingers to his mouth for a brief kiss before leaping to his saddle and picking his way stealthily from the French camp, leaving Valentina gasping with relief.

"Madame!" The shout jerked Valentina to her senses and she hurried round to the front of her tent again.

"They are here!" A pointed finger sent Valentina flying forward to join others who gathered as the shout went up and the French army trickled slowly back into camp.

The faces of the commanders were like graven images as they rode behind their king and Charles' face was slack and held no triumph as he led his soldiers between the tents.

The men were silent.

Just the tramp of their feet and the dull clop of the horses' hooves in the dust, the squeak of the wheels on the guns.

The few wounded men brought up the rear but there were no grins of relief to be safely back.

Valentina caught hold of Raoul's stirrup as he came level with her and she almost cried aloud as he turned dull empty eyes down to her. Thoughts of the Borgia fled as she asked tentatively. "Are you hurt Monsignor?"

His voice was harsh. "Not in my body, Valentina, not in my body."

She held up her hand and he clasped her fingers. "Forgive me. I am not fit company just now. Will you excuse me?"

She summoned a smile and a nod and he turned his destrier away in the direction of his own tent. She stepped back and allowed his horse to move past her.

Darkness came and still he did not come to her.

Alain brought her some food but she was too concerned about Raoul to take it.

"Where is Monsignor? Has he eaten?"

"He begs you to excuse him, Madame. He is not hungry."

"Not hungry?" Anxiety sharpened her voice then she tightened her lips determinedly.

"Have a meal prepared and send it to Monsignor's tent, Alain. But give me a short time alone with him first."

"Yes, Madame." His voice held respect, sure of her ability to heal whatever ailed the Lion.

Moving quickly and purposefully towards Raoul's quarters, she experienced a faint tremor of nerves only as she paused outside the entrance to his tent.

As she stood, hesitant, there was a crash and a curse as something was knocked to the floor. The edge of desperation in his voice sent her plunging through the opening. He swung beligerantly towards her but when he realised who it was who stood there, he made a great effort at control and sketched a bow.

"Madame. Welcome. I was not expecting you."

A pause.

"I came to see if you would eat with me? Are you

not hungry?"

"Eat! Madame, if I never eat again it will be too soon. My stomach is sick. Sick of blood and screaming and death. And you ask me if I am hungry?" He cursed again most foully and she flinched then caught at his sleeve as he turned away. She felt the muscles bunch beneath her fingers then relax as he sighed and passed his hand over his eyes.

"Very well. I will eat. If you will stay and eat here with me."

"With pleasure, Monsignor."

He tilted his head to her and she smiled with relief to see the familiar glint in the golden eyes. He reached out to trail his fingertips down the velvety bloom of her cheek, allowing his forefinger to continue down the side of her throat and along the delicate line of her collarbone. She closed her eyes at the sensation his caress aroused in her, swaying towards him to be caught in the powerful embrace which she had come to desire above all else.

"Oh! Your pardon Monseigneur, Madame..." It was Louis carrying a tray holding bowls of steaming food.

"Come in, Louis. You must be a reader of minds. Madame has scarcely talked me into having something to eat and here you are, with the food all prepared. Amazing!"

Valentina shot him a nervous, sidelong look and clenched her teeth at the sardonic raise to his brow.

Raoul waved Louis into the tent and towards a small table where he placed the tray and stood waiting to serve them.

"Thank you. You may go."

"Go, Monseigneur?"

"Yes. I shall wait on Madame this evening."

"Yes Monseigneur. Goodnight. Goodnight Madame."

Valentina inclined her head and muttered something and the page left.

Alone finally, they stared at each other then as Raoul took a step towards her there came another interruption. Alain's voice called for permission to enter, his tone edged with urgency. Raoul was exasperated but called his lieutenant in.

"Forgive me, Monseigneur, Madame, for intruding but the Borgia has escaped! The camp is up! The servants took food to his quarters and he is fled. His horse has gone and the guard denies all knowledge of it. They are questioning the guard now."

Valentina shuddered, well knowing what the

'questioning' would be like. She fought to keep her features calm. She must say nothing.

Raoul was looking at her curiously, seeming to see something in her which bothered him, then he turned back to Alain.

"The guard was not our responsibility this time. The duty was with de Brieur, therefore leave it to him to worry over the Borgia and make sure I am not disturbed again this night."

"Yes, Monseigneur. Goodnight."

Silence fell once more as the young lieutenant left them alone. Valentina fought down that sense of guilt and sat quietly in the chair which Raoul pulled out for her. He sat opposite her and poured the wine, raising his goblet to her and watching her strangely over the rim.

"I drink to you, my Valentina." His voice was deep and husky and held a note which puzzled her. "You are a clever woman, my love and I must make sure that I do not cross you again for I could not bear to lose you, no matter what you do. You will always hold my heart in your hands."

An image of Cesare Borgia making good his escape made her swallow hard then she smiled at Raoul and returned his salute with her cup.

They ate sparingly and drank deeply then the

night took on that dreamlike quality which overtook her every time this man made love to her. Reality was blurred into a kaleidoscope of colours, of warm sweet breath and caressing touch. She cried out his name, clutching him to her and raising herself to meet the demand in his body. He soothed her with a whisper and the feathering of his lips over her temple.

Shivers tremored her skin and her mouth sought his as he entered her then lay still for a moment, as though savouring their union. He pressed light kisses to the delicate skin below her ear and she surged against him, inviting the rhythm which grew like a tide as they took their pleasure of each other.

The agony and guilt within him eased as he felt her love enfolding him and it was with some sense of wonderment that he finally cradled her against him, whispering endearments which he had never thought to say to any woman.

Cesare Borgia thundered through the night pushing his exhausted horse to its limits in his desperate dash to return to Rome. His thoughts were with the sweet Florentine, wife of the Lion and he coveted her. Oh, how he coveted her!

CHAPTER X

Monte di San Giovanni smouldered in the distance as the French army continued its advance on Naples. Eyes were averted and heads bowed, many making the sign of the cross at their breast as they passed the tragic ruins of what had been a prosperous little town until it had sought to defy that hideous youth who was the King of France.

Raoul was riding with Valentina but he deliberately kept his gaze on his wife, refusing to even glance towards what he had helped destroy.

"How long until we reach the city?" Valentina distracted him.

"A few days, no more. Charles is expecting a welcome rivalling that which he received in Florence. I should think they will be too frightened to accord him anything else now."

Valentina ignored the remark. "They say Naples is utterly fascinating and that those who rule never want to leave."

That brought a smile. "The intention is to secure the place and then take up another crusade."

"Dear Mother of God! Cross to the land of the Infidels? He is surely mad."

"He will not do it. Already there are calls amongst his lords to return home. He will have no support. Also there are rumours that Cesare Borgia has managed to gather together an alliance of city states against us." He shook his head. "They would stand no chance of defeating us, no matter how many of them band together."

Valentina preferred not to talk of the Borgia. She was suffering pangs of guilt about allowing Cesare to escape unhindered and so she turned the conversation to her family. Soon she had her husband choking with laughter at some of the escapades she had got up to and when she told him how she had toyed with her father, Guido, over the money, he begged her to stop.

"I shall beware of upsetting you in future, have no doubt of that. I would not wish to come home and find a rat in my bed or some such dire revenge of yours, you can be sure."

Valentina spent the rest of the journey to that decadent city of Naples keeping her husband's mind off the terrible deed at Monte di San Giovanni. The rousing welcome from the Neapolitans cheered them all and their spirits were high when they moved into quarters vacated precipitously by the former Spanish rulers.

King Alfonso had fled so hastily that neither he nor any of his followers had even bothered to pack. The French fell on the discarded possessions like hounds on a fox and in the forefront was, of course, Alain d'Imoges. Valentina suddenly seemed to possess more silks and satins than she could ever possibly wear and even her jewel box became so full of valuables that a secret hiding place had to be found for it.

The city of Naples was like a great, voluptuous whore – a famous one it must be said but one which appealed immensely to the French and to their king. The Neapolitans had never been over fond of their Spanish rulers and the French found themselves feted in a style which surprised and delighted them.

In the palazzo overlooking the bay where Raoul and Valentina had finally settled in, the luxury and decadence was greatly appreciated. There was one room which was dedicated entirely to bathing. A huge circular bath, sunk into the floor had its inspiration from Moorish palaces and Valentina could not wait to see it filled with hot, scented water and lit by a greater number of candles than had ever illuminated the old Palazzo Velucci. She stayed in the water until it cooled and the skin on her fingers wrinkled then when she had dried herself she lavished her body with the various scented creams and lotions which had once been the pride of some Spanish noble's lady.

She was scarcely dressed when some instinct made her look up to see her husband leaning there against the doorway watching her. The fiercely possessive expression on his face made her stomach clench with anticipation and she waited, scarcely breathing, for him to come to her.

Raoul dismissed Louis with a flick of his fingers and he and Valentina were left alone.

The hangings of silk and gold, the spice scented air and the soft glow of candles created a touch of magic which stirred the blood and as Raoul turned his wife and bent his head to touch his lips to that soft, delicate spot at the nape of Valentina's neck, the shivers of desire which shook her were almost unbearable. Gentle fingers lifted the hair from her ear and his mouth sought the tender lobe, caressingly. Then he began to kiss, soft as a moth's breath at first but then more harshly until he was catching the flesh of her neck then her shoulders in his teeth. Valentina half-turned to protest, but her words were never spoken. His mouth was on hers, hot, urgent, and his hands were dragging at the fastenings of her gown. She gave a slightly hysterical laugh at the thought of another ruined dress and wondered why he had not come minutes earlier when she was already naked then she was frantically helping him to undress both herself and him.

Too desperate, suddenly, for gentleness Raoul lifted her high against him and thrust deep within her. He leaned her back against the silk covered wall and rested there for a moment, his mouth seeking her breast then running up and covering her mouth, whispering against her kiss, "I love you. Sweet Florentine, I love you with every breath I take. I think I have loved you since I saw you hanging from your balcony, laughing and scaring my horse half to death. If your father had not agreed to let me have you, I would have stolen you away anyway."

Valentina's world stood still. With his flesh inside her and his golden eyes on hers, beseeching and promising at the same time she was shaken by the enormity of the emotion that surged through her.

"I love you." She replied softly, almost shyly. He bent his head until his brow was against hers and then he took her with a hunger that left her in no doubt that indeed he would have done as he had said and stolen her away for his pleasure.

They sampled the delights of the city that had seduced princes and sultans alike as Charles settled down to enjoy his new domain, with a succession of pretty mistresses who scandalised even the French court.

To the north, his rivals were busy plotting his downfall.

They were not without help amongst Charles' own followers.

Heavily muffled in a dark cloak, Camille de Brieur waited nervously and impatiently in the rear of the lamp sellers shop. If it were not for the lure of the gold she could wish herself anywhere except in this foetid hole.

"Hsst!" The dramatic hiss made her jump and she turned angrily on Piero del Aguila, that indispensable servant of Cesare Borgia.

"Do not hiss at me so! You have the money?"

"You have the information?"

"You surely do not think I would be here if I did not?"

He grinned and ran an appreciative hand down her thigh. She dealt him a ringing slap and glared at him furiously so that he shrugged before handing over a bag which clinked to her satisfaction.

"Here!" The doeskin-wrapped tube was hidden away in del Aguila's cloak in seconds and before Camille could blink, he was gone.

Camille sneaked through to the front of the small shop and peered out then she drew back again with a curse.

Towards her, along the brightly lit street of stalls and shops, came Raoul de Baisleon and his wife, Valentina.

They were laughing together and teasing the shopkeepers as they begged them to enter their shops and sample their wares. Escorted by Alain d'Imoges and a group of heavily armed soldiers, the Lion of France was out to purchase trinkets for his wife. Necklaces and ear rings were held up for his inspection and finally he indicated to one lucky shopkeeper that he would enter his premises to choose something for Valentina.

Camille watched them with envy and hatred in

her heart, wishing that there was some way that she could destroy them and their happiness. The bag of gold moved against her leg where she had hidden it beneath her skirts and Camille suddenly smiled. Anyone seeing that smile would have been afraid.

Valentina was supremely happy. Raoul showered her with love and attention. Each time he saw her he had a gift of some sort for her and the matter became a joke between the two of them. Her jewels were the finest that Naples could offer and she was the envy of Charles' court.

Charles was content to enjoy the spoils of his captured domain and dallied in the fickle enticing kingdom of Naples as many conquerors had done before him. The summer moved on in a continuous round of pleasure and self-indulgence. His commanders followed his example. All but one.

The Lion of France continued to drill and exercise his men outside the walls of the city and it became an entertainment for the lords and ladies of Naples to sit in the shade and watch the French troops march and sweat in the hot sun. Charles was impressed and showered Raoul with favours and honours which aroused jealousy amongst the his brother commanders.

The king looked on in delight as he played his

favourite game of stirring up trouble amongst his lords.

Valentina could see what the king was up to.

"Charles is up to his old tricks, Monsignor. Be careful or you may find an assassin waiting in the dark for you one night."

"I am used to Charles and his amusements, so do not worry, my love. So long as I have you waiting in the dark for me at night, I shall not complain."

She smiled at his joke but still she worried. She was worried because Camille was smiling too much. The woman had gone from either ignoring Valentina or making nasty, hurtful remarks to her in front of as many people as possible, to being almost pleasant, almost friendly. Valentina was by no means a fool. She wondered what Camille was up to.

The following day a message came for Valentina from her friend, Etoile d'Erpignan.

"The ladies of the court have arranged a boating party, Madame. It is to take place tonight and it is to be a torchlit masque with music and entertainment out in the bay. A pontoon has been constructed with seats arranged for the ladies to watch the players."

Etoile's page could not keep the enthusiasm from his young face and Valentina, herself, felt excited at the promised spectacle. In Venice such masques were popular and the idea had caught on quickly here in Naples. The heat of the summer evenings lent themselves well to such entertainments.

"You may tell Madame d'Erpignan that I shall be delighted to accompany her and my thanks for thinking to invite me."

The page bowed and left and Valentina called her maid, Deodora, to help decide what she should wear. The plump, dark eyed maid chattered and fussed over her mistress with enthusiasm and Valentina enjoyed getting ready almost as much as she expected to enjoy the masque.

The sun set in a blaze of crimson and purple over the magnificently beautiful Bay of Naples. The multitude of torches which sprang to life almost rivalled the setting sun and their reflection in the waters of the Bay were a magical adjunct to the start of the masque, a play to music provided by some of the large gypsy population which thronged to Naples to profit from the French occupation.

Boats had ferried the ladies out to the wooden pontoon and the play took place on large flat punts on the water, a somewhat risky and fragile stage, thought Valentina. The waters of the Bay, although lit by the magical torches, were deep and cold this far out and, in the dark, anyone falling in would soon be lost.

Wine and food were passed around and the carnival atmosphere grew a little frenzied as the evening progressed. Most of the ladies were without their lords as were Valentina and Etoile, both their husbands having been called to one of Charles' interminable councils. A few of the local bravos had decided to climb onto the pontoon and flirt outrageously with the French ladies and the giggles and the occasional shriek gave evidence of something more than a little harmless flirtation here and there.

Etoile was drawn away by one of the players and Valentina was left alone briefly. She knelt and trailed her fingers in the water, thinking of Raoul, wishing he was with her, wondering what time Charles would allow his commanders to leave and return to their wives. Suddenly, a vicious shove in her back sent her falling forward into the darkness of the waters of the Bay.

She sank quickly, the skirts of her gown rapidly absorbing the water and acting as a weight to pull her down. Valentina fought like a demon to reach the surface, trying desperately not to swallow the great rushes of salt water which filled her eyes, her ears, her nose and her throat.

She surfaced briefly to a cacophony of noise, a shrill screaming and a jumble of shouts, lights bobbing in the dark then a voice in her ear.

"The rope, Madame. The rope!"

The rough thickness of rope was forced into her grasping fingers and she clung to it with the strength of a madwoman. She gasped the blessed air into her heaving lungs and kicked her legs, hampered by the clinging skirts of her gown, desperately trying to reach the safety of the boat.

The bravo who had dived in to help her was joined by others, eager hands more than willing to assist in the rescue of Madame de Baisleon. The rewards could be great.

Finally, thankfully, she closed her fingers over solid wooden gunwales and those aboard pulled her in.

Faces spun into focus then blurred again. Strangers, sailors who owned the boats, the man who had rescued her, dripping dark hair and smiling eyes. The anxious white features of Etoile d'Erpignan and, with awful clarity before she blacked out, the furious, tight lipped expression of Camille de Brieur.

Wrapped up in cloaks, Valentina was rushed

back to the palazzo and the little maid ordered water to be heated for the bath. "To ward off the chills. Most important."

In a daze Valentina was bathed and then rubbed down vigorously waving a hand several times for them to stop as she vomited up copious quantities of sea water. Finally, she was put to bed and then, as she laid her aching head on the soft pillow, she knew he had come into the room. His fingers caressed her hair and his lips were pressed to her brow and she drifted off into sleep content in the knowledge that Raoul was watching over her.

CHAPTER XI

"It was Camille."

He did not seem to believe her.

"Did you see her do it?"

"No. But I saw her face afterwards and she was furious that she had not succeeded in murdering me. And you know that it was she who tried to have me taken on the journey to Rome."

Raoul flinched at that then, sighing, he spread out his hands. "Without solid proof I cannot accuse the wife of a brother commander of trying to drown you or abduct you. Surely you must understand that?"

"She is still jealous. She still wants you and with me out of the way then she could have you again."

In a moment he was beside her, his hands gripping her shoulders, fingers biting deep as his anger surged. "You know that is not true! I could never consider taking that woman again. I was a blind fool to have become involved with her in the first place, I know that now. She has caused nothing but trouble. But this..." He shook his head. "I think you are wrong."

Valentina wrenched herself away from his grip, her own anger building now. "Oh, why will you not see? You may have finished with her but she is a dangerous woman and you are too soft headed to listen to me."

"Perhaps you are right, Madame. I have always been soft with women and that is my downfall. If you insist then I shall make a complaint but you must realise that this could cause us more trouble than it is worth."

His voice was cold and Valentina could hardly believe that he did not think it worth the trouble when she had almost died.

"Forget about it!" She turned away from him. "I would not wish to upset your rise to favour with your king. Forget it!"

There was a moment of silence while Raoul stared at her stiff back, confused, sorry that he had been so abrupt. But unsure how to mend things now. He bowed to that unrelenting spine.

"Very well, Madame. I shall see you this evening. The court is dining with the king. A formal affair so I shall collect you with a litter when you are ready."

She still did not turn or reply, so he left, exasperated, hoping that she would be in a better frame of mind by the evening.

Valentina was fuming with anger and still distressed by her narrow escape from drowning so that she could not understand his attitude. Surely, after all his sweet words and the passion of their lovemaking, he was not still hungry for the slut whom, she was convinced had tried to kill her?

No. She could not believe that. It was simply that he was blind to that woman's true capabilities and there lay the danger. How, though, could Valentina persuade him? Angering him was not the way, that was certain. A smile brightened her eyes. Now where was that new dress?

Charles was furious. His commanders were silent as he raged at the Pope and his son and all those who now were ranged against him.

"'Tis that miscreant bastard son of the Pope! Cesare Borgia is behind all this. Only he could have persuaded Milan to turn against me and turned this into almost a Holy War. A Holy War against the foremost ruler in Christendom!"

Charles' loose lips dribbled as he ranted and raved to his commanders in the Council chamber.

"Sire, we must retreat now. If we do not move soon then we will be completely cut off. Our men grow soft and idle in this place. Please, Sire, leave a garrison here and let us go home."

"Coward's talk, Sire. It seems the Lion has lost his taste for fighting since he married the Florentine." The sneering remark came from Etienne de Brieur and Raoul turned on him, white-faced, his hand reaching for his sword, which of course was not there. The two men stood eye to eye, glaring at each other.

"You question my courage, my honour?" The words came through gritted teeth and Etienne laughed in Raoul's face.

"Most certainly I question your honour."

For several moments more Raoul stared out the man whose wife he had bedded for so long, then he stood back, giving ground over this matter, guilt tightening his throat. There was a sigh, almost, from the assembled company and Charles, who had been watching the little scene with great enjoyment, was disappointed.

He drooped heavy lids over his bulging eyes and sat deep in thought for several moments.

"Mes Seigneurs. It has come to our attention that not all here are as loyal as they should be. Information is being passed to the Papal Court. A messenger was discovered on the road to the north bearing letters telling of our weakness here. How the heat of the southern sun is sapping our strength and our courage. Unfortunately the messenger... died... before he could be questioned thoroughly, but I warn you all to be on your guard for as you talk you may be talking to a traitor."

The commanders glanced uneasily at each other. Etienne de Brieur's face was like a mask, expressionless, only a single bead of sweat trickled from the side of his brow. They could imagine how the messenger had died – no doubt screaming for that death.

The king finally waved his dismissal and they left almost silently, half afraid to speak to a brother commander, more from fear that suspicion would be brought upon themselves than from fear of giving away information.

Raoul de Baisleon met his lieutenant of lancemen, Alain d'Imoges, in the courtyard and motioned to him not to speak. He waited until they were well away from the Palazzo before discussing the details of the council and the suspicions of the king, with the handsome young Frenchman.

"Yet who could do such a thing, Monseigneur? We are all men of one country here so who would betray his brothers to the likes of the Borgia?"

"Easy enough, Alain, if one needs something desperately. If debtors are knocking at the door, the lure of gold is often enough to make a man smother his principles and forget about his honour. Even a woman. Some men become so enamoured that they would do anything to gain a woman's favour, do anything she said in order to lay with her."

Alain glanced uneasily at his lord for there was a certain note in the Lion's voice which, if one did not know any better, might indicate that he had been there, experienced that. But then that was ridiculous.

It was dusk as the Lion of France returned to his quarters and he was tired and dispirited after the long day of argument and speculation. That moment when de Brieur had challenged him had sickened him. It was he, Raoul de Baisleon, who had been in the wrong and he could understand the man's hatred. He wondered if Valentina was still angry with him for not accusing Camille de Brieur of attempted murder. He could well do without dining with the king and with all the posturing and boot-licking which always accompanied such events.

As he approached that part of the palazzo where lay his quarters, his hand suddenly dropped to his sword hilt as a shadow moved in the darkness.

"What, Monseigneur? Are you afraid of a mere woman?"

Raoul stared in surprise and consternation at Camille de Brieur. She had not bothered so much with him these last months and he had assumed that she had forgotten her obsession with him. The stinging confrontation with Camille's husband had hurt both his pride and his sense of honour. He wanted nothing more to do with this woman.

She moved close to him, allowing her cloak to fall open and reveal that she wore a dress beneath it that certainly left nothing to the imagination. Raoul swallowed a curse and checked the corridor ahead to see if anyone was about, more to protect him from Camille than to discover them together.

"What are you doing here, Madame? Your husband would kill us both were he to discover you here."

"You were not so careful of my husband's feelings in the past, Raoul. I just thought that you might be feeling bored and in need of a little diversion. After all, a little variety in life quickens the palate."

"My palate is not jaded as yet, Madame, nor is it likely to become so. I thought that you understood that our relationship was well over."

Camille paled at his words. She had thought to remind Raoul that she was still available and although she had watched the Lion and his wife absorbed in each other, she knew from long experience that couples often tired of each other in a short time. It seemed that this time she had judged badly. She knew that Valentina suspected that she, Camille, had been the one to push her into the water the other night and when Raoul had done nothing about it then she had hoped that his reasons were quite obvious.

She tried again.

"Raoul, my darling, consider. You know I have always loved you. If my father had not married me to Etienne against my will, I would have been so happy to be your wife. I swear I would never have looked at another man if I could have had you."

He gave a short, mocking laugh.

"My dear Camille, you could no more stay faithful to one man than my horse could sprout wings and fly like a bird. I could never ask someone to be my wife in whose fidelity I could not absolutely believe."

Stung by his contempt, Camille's voice rose in bitter accusation. "You are not so virtuous yourself, Monseigneur. You thought nothing of taking another man's wife in adultery, for all your high principles."

His answer was a whiplash to her bruised pride, the image of her husband challenging him, still stinging his conscience.

"Madame, your body was anyone's for the taking. I did but ease my lust on one who acted the bitch in heat. Now get out of my way and do not seek to ply your trade with me nor to threaten my wife again or life could become most unpleasant for you."

For several moments she stared at him, her mouth opening but her fury too great for words then with a strangled shriek of rage, Camille fled from the man who had so humiliated her. All she could think of now was revenge. He would be sorry. Oh, yes. He would be very sorry.

Valentina had spent a long time getting ready to accompany Raoul that evening. Her bath had been scented and leisurely and Deodora, the maid, had massaged the perfumed creams into her mistress's skin until she glowed. The choice of gowns occupied them for quite some time and they changed their minds again and again. Finally Valentina was dressed in an ivory silk gown which emphasised her tiny waist, the skirts billowing out and shimmering with the tiny diamonds scattered amongst the folds. Instead of a formal headdress, her hair had been twisted and coiled and confined with a gold net set with diamonds. Echoing that brightness were long diamond drops in her ears and a tear-shaped single diamond hung tantalisingly between the cleft of her breasts.

Valentina looked breathtaking and as she descended the steps to where Raoul waited for her, she was more than delighted with the admiration she saw in his eyes.

"Valentina, you do full justice to my gifts. I am enchanted."

He raised both her hands to his lips and then helped her into the litter which waited there.

It was a bumpy ride to Charles' quarters through the twisting streets of Naples and Valentina pulled aside the curtains of the litter a little to look out at the crowds of passing Neapolitans. Although the majority of people clapped and waved at the litter and the men on horseback, through her peephole she saw the odd furtive gesture of hatred. A woman raising her index finger in contempt as the troops passed and a man spitting foully in the hoofprints of Raoul's horse.

She let drop the curtain and sat back, her mood sobered a little by what she had seen then she was distracted by the bump as the litter was set down and the curtains were pulled aside once more for Raoul to take her hand and help her out.

The splendour of the former King Alfonso's court took Valentina's breath away. No wonder Charles did not want to leave, did not want to give up all of this, she thought. She had been awed by the magnificence of Rome but the frescoed walls and ceilings of this palazzo and the beauty of the marble statuary, the gleam of gold leaf and the drape of silk hangings was beyond her imagining.

Making her curtsey before Charles, she smiled up at the young king, used to his lascivious stare by now then as she turned away at her husband's side it was a shock when she caught Camille's glare of pure hatred. Refusing to look away, Valentina returned that basilisk stare with a challenge and fearlessness which aroused a flicker in those blue eyes for a moment.

"Madame?" Raoul's whisper distracted Valentina

and she put Camille out of her mind and concentrated solely on the man she loved.

The festivities went on long into the night and Valentina danced and flirted with her husband with a strange sense of urgency which she could not explain. He gave her his undivided attention and it seemed to her that he had forgotten even the existence of Camille de Brieur.

In the lonely hour before dawn, someone made a stealthy inspection of the quarters assigned to the Lion and his lady. It was so dark that it was difficult to see exactly what they wanted but eventually, in the dressing room used by Raoul for his private correspondence, where he kept letters and accounts relating to the running of his lands in France, they discovered a small chest. Innocuous enough, it was full of letters and plain writing materials and it was the work of only a moment to secrete a couple of crumpled pieces of parchment at the bottom of the chest, where they would not be noticed except by someone searching for them. Once the deed was done, the secret someone left quickly and as silently as they had arrived.

CHAPTER XII

Cesare Borgia was almost a happy man.

The information provided by Camille de Brieur had proved most instrumental in persuading those Seigneurs still hesitating about taking on the might of the French army, to agree that perhaps it might be possible to oppose that feared killing machine. There was still a little arm-twisting to be done, but then Cesare was an expert at that sort of thing. The one thing that still haunted him was his unassuaged desire for the wife of Raoul de Baisleon. If only there was some way to tempt her into his power.

In Naples, the Lion of France longed to return home with his wife. The adventure promised by the Italian campaign had become boring now and the destruction of Monte di San Giovanni had sickened him. Not that he was not used to death and destruction, but it had been all so totally unnecessary.

He and Valentina were absorbed in each other. He continued to find constant delight in his wife, in her sense of humour and in her love and desire for him. Camille de Brieur was long forgotten.

The weather was hot and sultry. A new material had been discovered by Valentina in the markets of Naples. Soft and light, it came from the East and it made up into the coolest and most comfortable of dresses. It has to be said that they were a little revealing of a lady's figure but the desire in Raoul's gaze when he looked at her made that into a virtue for the Lady de Baisleon.

"Madame, Monseigneur wonders whether you would be interested in an excursion to some ancient ruins just outside the city. We would need to leave before the heat becomes unbearable but we could rest there at noon time and return here just before dusk."

To Valentina, any time spent with her husband was time well spent and so she nodded eagerly.

"Certainly, Alain. Tell Monseigneur that I shall be delighted to accompany him as soon as he is ready."

A letter had arrived from Bianca Velucci that

morning, informing her daughter that the monies Valentina had sent to the Florentine bankers had arrived safely and thanking her for her generosity. Two more pages told of the betrothal of the twins Lucrezia and Cara and, miracle of miracles, also of Medina, something of which her mother had, frankly, despaired. Even Guido, her father, had made one or two good investments and he was so proud of himself that Bianca thought he would burst.

"It is all thanks to you, my dearest daughter and my fervent wish is that you are happy with your French lord and that, perhaps, it would be possible for you to visit us on the return of the French forces to the north on their way home to France."

Valentina sighed at that. She suddenly missed her mother and sisters and even her father. She would ask Raoul about the possibility of a future visit. In the meantime she must choose something suitable to wear for their jaunt to the fascinating past that had been left to fall into ruin.

Raoul watched her as she descended the steps towards him. That gown really was a little immodest in its transparency but he could not deny himself the pleasure of lusting after her soft curves, faintly visible through the drifts of material.

She smiled up at him, well aware of the effect she was having on him. Perhaps they would be doing more than just exploring old ruins this afternoon. The anticipation made her shiver.

"Hold! In the name of the king, stay where you are and do not touch your weapons!"

The shout from the gates of the palazzo stunned them all. They watched in amazement as King Charles' Swiss infantry, led by Etienne de Brieur, swarmed into the courtyard and rapidly disarmed Raoul's men.

"You are under arrest, Monseigneur de Baisleon. Your sword, if you please."

Alain surged forward with an oath but Raoul halted him with an upraised hand.

"Arrested, Monseigneur? On what charge?"

There was a moment of anticipatory silence and de Brieur could not disguise the note of satisfaction in his voice as he replied.

"The charge is treason. Treason, Monseigneur."

"No! How can you say such a thing? Who makes these charges? Are you mad? Or is it that lunatic of a king who can believe such nonsense?" Valentina did not care what she said in defence of her lord. She shouted her questions into the smug features of Etienne de Brieur. Raoul took hold of her, pulling her away from the man who had come for him and looked to Alain.

"See to Madame's safety. Make sure no-one enters her apartments no matter what. And do not worry. The truth of this will out."

The reassurance was for Valentina's benefit but Raoul's face was grim. Once the accusations had been made it was going to be very difficult to prove himself innocent.

"Your sword, Monseigneur." De Brieur repeated his request, holding out his hand.

Raoul ignored him, unbuckling his sword and handing it, not to de Brieur, but to the embarrassed captain of the Swiss guard who stood to one side.

Etienne sneered and shrugged. What did it matter? De Baisleon was dead whoever he surrendered to.

"Search the buildings. And make sure you miss nothing."

Those words made Raoul frown. Camille's husband seemed too sure of himself. There was something here which whispered a warning in Raoul's brain. At the moment, however, there was nothing he could do but wait and see what transpired.

Valentina called his name, unbelieving,

bewildered, desperate.

Alain shushed her consolingly. "It will be alright, Madame. No-one could ever believe Monseigneur guilty of treason. There has been a mistake."

Firmly he led her away, although her tragic gaze never left her husband, standing between two of the guards who had come to arrest him.

Once in her chamber, Valentina calmed. There must be something she could do. She was certainly not prepared to sit and wait, perhaps wait to hear that her husband was to be executed. No. She would go and see Charles.

"Alain. Request an audience with the king. We must speak to him. Find out why he has accused Monseigneur and persuade him that he has made a mistake."

"Very well, Madame."

"Deodora. The red dress. Let no-one think that we are in despair."

They waited for two hours before a reply came from the king.

Madame de Baisleon was to wait on His Majesty after dinner that evening. She was to dine at the court.

"He likes to play the voyeur. He will expect you to be distraught and red-eyed, Madame."

"Well he is in for a surprise, Alain. As are they all."

Truly they were surprised.

Valentina looked magnificent in the red dress and she held her head proudly as Alain escorted her to her chair. Her gaze, inevitably, met that of Camille de Brieur. Avid, triumphant, it made Valentina feel sick, yet she met that look with a cold contempt which caused Camille to pale.

The food tasted of dust and Valentina ate automatically, chewing and swallowing without knowing what she did.

Her mind was busy considering the import of Raoul's arrest. She did not believe for one moment that he was a traitor. Why should Camille and her pathetic husband be so triumphant? Camille's hatred had been obvious from the first moment that Valentina had met her and it could only have been fuelled by the obvious love which Raoul had displayed towards his wife, particularly recently.

Of course Valentina knew nothing of that dark meeting between Raoul and Camille which had resulted in the spurning of the Frenchwoman and her total humiliation.

There had been Camille's attempt to drown Valentina. More. The guard on Cesare Borgia had been with de Brieur on the day he had escaped. Her mind ferreted busily through everything she knew. She must see Charles. There must be something more. Charles would never act precipitously in a case like this. There must be something more.

At last the meal was over and she was admitted to the king's audience chamber, leaving an anxious Alain waiting outside.

Valentina curtsied gracefully before the king who regarded her solemnly for several seconds before speaking.

"Madame, before you say anything, I must make it clear that the situation is most serious. We have known for some time that we have a traitor in our midst, passing information to those who desire our downfall. The Seigneur de Baisleon has been accused by a brother commander and although I am as shocked and disbelieving as you must be yourself, I must act on information such as this for my own credibility and the security of all within my power. You understand my position?"

"Sire, I understand the position very clearly and I am grateful to you for granting me this chance to speak with you alone. I wish only to know two things; who is my husband's accuser? And what proof of guilt do you have?"

Charles' loose lips pulled into a smile at her tone. No weeping, wailing female this, to beg indulgence, but one who was prepared to fight and one who clearly believed her husband innocent.

"The one who accused the Lion is the Seigneur de Brieur." Charles paused to see the effect of this disclosure but Valentina showed no surprise, merely giving a small nod as though to confirm something she already knew.

"The proof is here. These letters were found in your husband's chamber and they are clearly replies to letters which have contained vital information about everything discussed in Council with my commanders, information which could only be known to those commanders."

Valentina took the two squares of parchment from Charles and scanned them briefly. Charles watched admiringly. What a pity this woman was so obviously devoted to the Lion.

"Sire, it seems to me that a great deal of evidence hangs on the word of the Seigneur de Brieur. Anyone could have slipped into my husband's quarters and placed these incriminating documents where they could so easily be found. Do you really think that a man of my husband's worth would be so foolish as not to conceal such damning evidence where it would never be found?"

"That is true, Madame. But why should de Brieur go to all this trouble to get rid of your husband?"

"Come now, Sire. You well know of my husband's former relationship with Camille de Brieur. Everyone knows of it. Why not de Brieur himself? Jealousy is a poisonous emotion."

"But to go so far? He would be aware of the fate of such a traitor. It would not be an easy death."

Valentina paled but clenched her teeth in an effort at control.

"And tell me, Madame. Where would de Brieur obtain the incriminating evidence? A forgery would not be possible. These letters bear the seal of the Borgia."

Valentina held Charles' eyes and spoke very deliberately.

"Sire, where did the responsibility for the guard lie on the night of Cesare Borgia's escape from the French?"

Charles frowned then as the thought took root he leaned back in his chair and placed his fingertips together, regarding them broodingly for several moments as Valentina stood waiting, her heart thumping. Please let him see! Surely it was obvious?

Charles whispered almost to himself.

"The guard was with de Brieur that day. Hmm. A coincidence? Perhaps not."

Charles sank once more into thought whilst hope rose in Valentina's breast.

"Madame, you have most certainly raised doubts in my mind, even if I was not doubtful of the Lion's guilt before. However, I must have more than mere speculation. I must be able to say to my commanders, I am certain the Lion is innocent and de Brieur is guilty because of this and this. I cannot say it is because the Lion's wife tells me that Cesare Borgia's guard was de Brieur's man."

"But Sire, what more can I say? What more can I do?"

The first sign of her distress started to show. Her voice cracked and her lip trembled.

"Madame, I do not know. All I know is that I must have more than mere words to show my commanders that their security lies with more than my fondness for a pretty face."

Valentina turned her back to the king for a moment, fighting for control and thinking frantically of what she might say or do to convince Charles to free her husband.

Suddenly a desperate idea came to her. The danger would be great, the risk unthinkable, but it was the only way. She turned back to Charles, her chin jutting with determination, her voice low but controlled.

"Time, Sire. I need time. There is something I must do but I must have time."

Charles wiped away a dribble of saliva from his chin with the heel of his hand and considered.

"How much time?"

"Two weeks." That scarcely give her enough time.

Charles shook his head. "I must have something before that. The most I can give you is ten days. Then you must have such evidence that none could dispute it."

"Very well, Sire. Ten days. I thank you."

Valentina curtsied and turned to leave. As she reached the door Charles' hoarse voice reached her.

"Madame."

She turned.

"Good luck. And may God aid you." She would need it, he added silently to himself.

She acknowledged his words with a strained smile and then left the room.

Ten days! It was not enough! It would have to be enough! She had no time to waste.

Alain caught up with her anxiously as she almost

ran from the palazzo of the Spanish kings.

"Madame, what did he say? Is there a chance?"

Valentina gave a short laugh. "Oh yes, Alain, there is a chance. But it is so slim... I..." She stopped and swallowed hard at the thought of what she must do then she gave her orders.

"A troop of men, Alain. Your very best and most experienced. Within the hour, mounted and ready. A horse for me also. The fastest horses you can find and we will need spare mounts too."

Alain hesitated, puzzled at her intentions yet convinced that anything she did would be to help the Lion.

"Alain, will you hurry? Time is our enemy."

"Yes, Madame."

Alain ran to his horse. Valentina's urgency now gripped him also and, clapping his heels to the animal's sides, he clattered away to where their men were quartered.

As Valentina stooped to enter her litter, a cloaked figure was suddenly beside her.

"Yes. Go, you bitch. Leave him to his fate and complete the comedy. You have brought this upon him and now you make your escape. Do not worry. I shall go and comfort him in his dark and lonely cell."

Valentina stepped back, shocked, as Camille de Brieur hissed her invective then a surge of such rage gripped her that before she knew what she was doing she had grasped Camille by the neck of the cloak and pushed her hard against the litter. The litter bearers gaped as their mistress turned into the deadly fury before them.

"Do you think I shall allow you to get away with your foul plan? If he dies do you imagine I shall allow you to survive? No Madame. You underestimate me. You and your traitor husband both. I shall not rest. I shall not sit back and leave him to die. Such is not my mettle."

The fingers at Camille's throat tightened and she gasped with fear at the sudden strength of this slim woman before her then with a supreme effort born of panic she tore herself from Valentina's grasp and fled, almost falling in her haste to escape.

When she had gone, Valentina's strength drained away and she leaned trembling against the litter. A bearer moved to help her and she almost collapsed onto the seat of the litter, tilting back her head against the soft cushions and allowing the tears to fall for the first time since Raoul's arrest.

By the time the litter bearers turned into the courtyard of the palazzo which had been such a happy place for Valentina over the past months, Alain was waiting for her with a bunch of hard looking men grouped behind him. Valentina inspected them closely and was satisfied. A more vicious looking lot would be difficult to find.

"Madame, what do you intend? Where are we going?"

She did not answer immediately but picked up her skirts and hurried to her chamber. Leaving the young lieutenant fretting outside, she changed into travelling clothes and was back with him in moments.

"Madame, please. Where are we headed?"

Valentina shook back her hair and spoke quietly but with deadly purpose.

"Alain, I go to the Borgia!"

The lieutenant was stunned. "Madame. You cannot! It is madness. How will you get there? He would not see you. More likely to have us all murdered. Why should he help us? I tell you it is madness!"

"It is the only way. Cesare Borgia owes me a favour and I intend to collect. Now come, stop gaping. We have very little time."

Short of knocking his mistress on the head, there was no way he could stop her and so Alain d'Imoges followed the wife of the Lion of France into the night for a rendezvous with one of his lord's deadliest enemies.

When they had gone, the emptiness of the torchlit courtyard was frightening in its silence.

CHAPTER XIII

They rode through the night. They rode until their beasts flagged under them and Alain reached across to catch hold of Valentina's bridle.

"Madame, we must call a halt. If our horses founder we shall never reach Rome."

He was right. Valentina pulled her exhausted mount to a halt.

"We have only ten days, Alain, to get there and back and to persuade Cesare Borgia to help us. We can stop only to rest the horses for we must cover ground that took the army four weeks to travel, in four days!"

Alain shook his head.

"It can be done, Madame, but only if we sprout wings."

The men were rubbing down the lathered horses

and taking a drink. Valentina sagged against her own horse as the groom saw to it and wondered whether she, herself, had the strength to journey so far, so fast. But then she had no choice.

Staring up at the starlit sky, she thought of Raoul, locked away, unaware of where she was and what she intended to do. The risk she took was very great and there was no guarantee that she would come out of it with what she needed, what she wanted. She needed incontrovertible proof that it was de Brieur who was the traitor and that he had falsely accused her husband.

Would Cesare do it? And if he did, what would he want in exchange? For Valentina was no fool. She knew that she would not get something for nothing from the Borgia, no matter what he owed her.

"Mount up!" Alain gave the order, assisting Valentina to mount her horse and leading off once more into the night, towards the north.

They did it in four days but only just.

They were attacked twice but their men were hard, experienced fighters and they dealt with the brigands who fancied their chance with a lone, lightly escorted woman, almost contemptuously.

It was different as they approached Rome and were stopped by a force larger than their own, heavily armed and obviously professional soldiers.

As they were surrounded and her men bunched around Valentina protectively, she cried out, shouting the one name which she knew would stop any attack.

"Cesare Borgia! Madonna Valentina de Baisleon to see Cesare Borgia! Attack us at your peril!"

The man leading the opposition could hardly believe his ears. The Velucci girl! The wife of the Lion of France asking for Cesare Borgia!

Piero del Aguila could not keep the grin from his face as he rode next to Valentina.

"And to what do we owe this pleasure, Madonna?"

"That is my business, Captain."

That wiped the grin from his face and he consoled himself with the thought of the reward that would be his when he escorted Valentina into the presence of his master.

If Cesare Borgia was surprised to see her, then he hid it well. A thin dark cropped beard now outlined his jaw and his eyes were, if possible, more secretive but otherwise he was the same... cool, calculating, a little sly.

"Madonna Valentina, this is such pleasure. I never thought to see you here again. What can I do for you?"

Did nobody come to this man except to ask for favours?

Valentina pushed aside the thought. Why else was she here but to collect a debt?

"Monsignor, you read me right. I have come for your help. You are the only person I can turn to and I beg that you will not refuse me."

Cesare Borgia's brows rose and his eyes became speculative. He could scarce believe his luck. The very woman he would have killed to possess was here and begging a favour from him. Had the Lion of France discarded her? If so then Cesare was more than willing to look after her. His heart thumped at the thought of possessing her but the expression he assumed was sympathetic. He was far too crafty to allow his true feelings to show.

"Wait one moment, Madonna. Will you not sit down? You are exhausted. I shall send for some refreshment."

Valentina did indeed feel as though the ground was heaving beneath her. The travel and anxiety had taken their toll and her stomach was behaving crazily.

She almost collapsed onto a seat and the Borgia removed her cloak, his fingers lingering covetously at the slim column of her neck before the servant arrived with a flagon of wine and he moved away to fill a cup for her.

He watched her as she recovered a little, and he felt again the surge of desire which overtook him every time she was near him. Holy Cross! He could take her here and now, on the floor. There would never be anyone to come to her help. Who would dare disturb him? Reluctantly, he fought away the temptation as she looked up at him. One thing he was sure of. Now that she was here, in his power, she would most certainly not leave.

Valentina put down her empty cup and prepared to make her request.

"Monsignor, my husband has been arrested for treason against his king. Proof of his guilt has been most adequately manufactured by the Signor de Brieur and his wife, Madonna Camille. King Charles, himself, does not believe in my husband's guilt, but he needs more than suspicions to lay before his commanders so that they do not think he acts from favouritism. He has given me ten days, of which only six are left, to bring evidence that it is de Brieur who is the traitor and not Raoul."

There was silence after this rush of speech and Valentina watched the Borgia's expression intently.

He, however, was past master at hiding what he was thinking. His lids veiled his eyes as he spoke.

"But I do not see how I can help, Madonna. If, as you say, de Brieur is my informant then I am hardly likely to provide you with evidence to dispose of him. How then would I know my enemy's movements? Particularly at such a dangerous time."

Valentina's heart sank. Had she taken this desperate chance for nothing? Was Raoul to die after all?

Her voice trembled although she tried hard to control it.

"Monsignor, let us not forget that if it were not for me, you might not now be here to receive information from de Brieur and plot accordingly."

Cesare Borgia smiled thinly. Here was suddenly a chance to have her. If not exactly willingly then certainly without violence.

"Ah. I wondered when you would raise that point Madonna. Very well. Suppose I were to help you, what do I get in return for losing my spy in the enemy camp?"

Valentina was at a loss. She had nothing to give him. He had riches enough by all accounts. And power. She shook her head.

"Monsignor, I have nothing which could be of

value to you. I do not know what I could offer."

"Do you not, Valentina, do you not? Do you then think so little of yourself? Do you not think that what you have to give is the thing that is most truly your own?" Cesare watched her, amused.

Bewilderment clouded her mind for only a moment before she understood with blinding clarity what he wanted.

"You want me, Monsignor? But why? I am not so special. I am married and cannot bring you alliances or even land. When you take me you take only my body, nothing more.

"Valentina, you underestimate your appeal. Come then, you understand me. Is it a bargain? If I help you to prove the Lion's innocence, will you return to me and become my mistress?" He watched her as a cat watches a mouse, sure of himself. What else could she do but agree? He almost laughed aloud at the way things had turned his way.

"Until such time as you tire of me? And I am sure you will tire of me."

"Probably. Eventually. But until then, Madonna..?"

What else could she do but agree? And when the Borgia tired of her? What then? She would not think of it. Her need, Raoul's need, was now. She had no choice.

"Very well, Monsignor..."

"Cesare."

"Very well... Cesare. I agree. But I must go back to Charles with the evidence. When my husband's freedom is certain, I shall return here, to you."

Cesare moved forward and took her hand, raising her fingers to his lips and kissing them lingeringly.

"You and your men will rest here tonight. I shall arrange for certain documents to be in your possession at first light and I shall expect you back here within the fortnight."

Valentina merely nodded. She was so exhausted now that everything seemed unreal and she felt sick again. Fighting off the nausea and clinging to the thought that she would have the means to save Raoul, she allowed herself to be put to bed like a child by the maidservant Cesare provided.

The next morning, Alain and the men were ready and waiting as Valentina descended to the courtyard with a packet of letters concealed beneath her bodice. Each letter unmistakably bore de Brieur's signature and seal and tied up so obviously with the two letters found in Raoul's room.

It was more, much more than Valentina had expected. She had no qualms over the fate of the

Lord de Brieur, for after all, if it had not been for him and his plotting she would not now be looking forward to becoming the mistress of the most dangerous man of the time.

Cesare stood at the side of her horse when she was mounted and took her hand.

"Farewell for now, Madonna. I have arranged an escort for your return. They will accompany you to the border of Naples and await you there. Good luck, Madonna."

Valentina looked down into the warm brown eyes, holding indulgence now, and a little of the horror fluttering at the back of her mind receded. She smiled.

"Farewell, Cesare." She used his name deliberately. "My thanks. My most heartfelt thanks."

She felt Alain's stare but ignored it.

They set out at the gallop. Their own troop was now reinforced by twenty of Cesare's own men led by the indispensable Piero del Aguila.

When they crossed the border of Naples, passing the still, accusing ruins of Monte de San Giovanni, Piero sat his horse watching as Valentina and her French escort rode out of sight. He wondered if she would return.

Alain had asked no questions. He was satisfied that Valentina had, somehow, acquired whatever she needed to prove Raoul's innocence. He wondered why the Borgia's men waited at the border.

They made it back to the city with no time to spare. A distraught Louis awaited them.

"Madame! Monseigneur is brought before the king and council to answer the charges against him."

"Not a man to waste time, this king." Valentina murmured grimly. "Do not worry, Louis. I have here Monsignor's reprieve. Alain, take the packet of letters straight to the king and tell him I succeeded in providing proof to satisfy the most demanding of his critics."

Without hesitation, without stopping to ask why his lady did not take the letters herself, Alain left hastily to do as she commanded.

The door closed behind him and Valentina was left, staring into space, facing alone what she now had to do. No time to think about it. She packed a few things then stopped. She stripped off her jewellery, keeping only the signet ring with the snarling lion's head with which Raoul had married her then left, closing the door on the empty room behind her.

Alain faced King Charles triumphantly.

"We are only just in time, Sire, it seems."

Charles looked uncomfortable but a king makes no excuses.

"You have fresh evidence?"

"Most certainly, Sire. From the Borgia himself."

Etienne de Brieur paled and his fingers sought the hilt of his sword.

Raoul's head jerked up and the golden eyes regained their glow.

Alain handed the packet of letters to the king and tension mounted as he read in silence. When he had finished he folded the papers and cocked an eyebrow to the captain of his guard. The man stiffened to attention.

"Mes Seigneurs, this makes most interesting reading. It seems that we were mistaken in thinking that it was the Lion who is the traitor. I did not think a lion would act the jackal and these documents prove me right."

Charles paused and his protuberant eyes scanned the uncomfortable commanders about him. Not one had not felt a slight pleasure at the apparent downfall of this man they considered the king's favourite. Now, however, they were doubtful and mistrustful once more. If it was not the Lion, then who was the traitor?

The question did not long remain unanswered.

De Brieur cracked under the pressure.

He jumped to his feet, his chair crashing to the floor behind him and leaped for the door.

Charles' guard captain did not wait for the king's signal. He had never believed in the Lion's guilt and before de Brieur could reach the door, half a dozen guards blocked his escape.

With sword bared, unheard of in the king's council, de Brieur turned, snarling, at bay.

The commanders sat as if turned to stone. Raoul fastened that cold, menacing stare on the man who had so nearly caused his dishonour and death. De Brieur swallowed convulsively but raised the point of his sword. Raoul's husky voice was even. "Alain, your sword!"

The lieutenant of lancemen did not even glance at his king for permission. The sword whispered from its sheath and was cast through the air to be caught by the sure grip of the Lion of France.

Charles sat back in his chair and held off the guard with an upraised hand. Perhaps it was better this way.

Raoul advanced softly and almost lazily, the

point of the sword weaving a fascinating pattern before the eyes of Etienne de Brieur. As the Lion closed on him, de Brieur gave a shout of defiance and leaped forward, raising his sword and bringing it down in a vicious arc at the Lion's head.

It met only steel.

Raoul did not even seem shaken by the heavy impact as de Brieur's sword slid away on the blade of his own. The two men circled warily for a moment before de Brieur attacked again, desperation giving him strength and for several minutes Raoul was hard put to stave off the rain of heavy blows to which his enemy subjected him.

Finally de Brieur fell back and paused for a moment, gasping for air. Raoul was not even breathing hard. The hours of battle practice which had so amused the Neapolitans now showed their worth and terror gripped the heart of de Brieur as Raoul hefted his weapon and stalked in for the kill.

The traitor reeled back under the relentless onslaught until, with a cry, his sword was beaten from his hand and he stumbled to lie helpless on the steps before the king's throne. Raoul's swordpoint wavered at his throat for an instant before the Lord de Baisleon gave a sigh and raised his eyes to his king.

"Your traitor, Sire."

Charles pulled his loose mouth into a smile of acknowledgement and at a sign the guard captain motioned several of his men to take the now quivering form of the Lord de Brieur from the chamber.

"Well now, my Lion, you are to be congratulated."

"Thank you, Sire."

"I would that such a lady were mine, Monseigneur. Worth her weight in jewels. I hope that you find a suitable reward for her efforts."

"Sire?"

It was the first time Charles had seen his most able commander at a loss and he chuckled with delight.

"Did you not know? Madame de Baisleon obtained these documents to prove your innocence. I do not know how, or from where, but you have your wife to thank for your freedom. No doubt your lieutenant will provide you with all the details. In the meantime, my compliments to Madame. My most heartfelt compliments. You may go."

"Thank you, Sire."

Raoul and his lieutenant bowed deeply and left the king still chortling to himself and gleefully anticipating the end of the Lord de Brieur.

Raoul said nothing as they reached the cool air of the courtyard and Alain sent a groom running for his lord's horse.

They waited.

Raoul took a deep breath and raised his eyes to the deep velvet blue of the midnight sky. The glint of the stars made him think of Valentina's eyes and his mind turned over what the king had said.

The horses arrived and the two men swung a little wearily into their saddles. Alain felt as if he had not been off a horse for years.

"Well, Alain. Now you can explain to me exactly what the king meant concerning Madame and how come I owe her my life.

By the time they reached the palazzo, Raoul had been regaled with all that had happened since his arrest. He had listened silently until Alain had finished and he was still silent as they dismounted and a jubilant Louis had led their horses away.

Raoul turned his steps towards Valentina's room, a little puzzled that she had not come out to greet him. He paused at the door and could not understand the feeling that turned his stomach to water. He gave a short laugh as he realised that the strange emotion was nervousness! The Lion of

France, nervous at seeing a woman, his wife, a woman who had, without doubt, saved his honour and his life.

He took a breath and opened the door, stopping as though he had walked into a wall as darkness met him.

Inexplicable panic gripped him and he shouted for light.

"Louis! Alain! Lights quickly! Bring some lights!"

As he waited in the dark his mind invented nightmares of what he might find. Had Camille contrived something? She had not been arrested so far as he knew.

The reality was almost a relief.

The three men stared about the empty chamber in disbelief. Raoul clenched his fist.

"Search the palazzo. Question everyone. She must be somewhere."

A half an hour later a trembling groom knelt before Raoul.

"I did not think Monseigneur. Madame commanded, I obeyed."

"Which way did she go?"

"I do not know Monseigneur. Perhaps the guard at the gate?"

"They took the road to the north, towards the

border, Monseigneur. Madame and three or four bravos who met her in the night."

The Lord de Baisleon spent three days searching the kingdom of Naples but no trace of his wife did he find.

CHAPTER XIV

Four of del Aguila's men were waiting for her on the road out of the city.

Valentina waved away the guard who had accompanied her from the palazzo.

"My thanks. My escort is here now. You may go."

"Yes, Madame." The Frenchman did not like the look of the bravos in the dark, their cloaks pulled close about them and their caps down over their brow. He watched as the lady disappeared with them into the night.

Over the border, Cesare's lieutenant waited anxiously and when Valentina and his men finally were sighted, Piero heaved a sigh of relief. Even he would not have dared to return to his master without this prize. The Borgia had made that quite clear.

Valentina fell from her horse into del Aguila's arms, losing consciousness as he caught her. He panicked at her paleness, ordering wine to be heated and stoking up the fire to warm her as he laid her down in a nest of cloaks.

"Any sign of pursuit?"

"None, Messire. I do not think that they even realise that the lady has gone."

"Good. When she has recovered a little we shall move camp, perhaps towards San Giovanni. They would not search for her there I think. Then when we are sure all is clear, take the coast road home."

He fussed over Valentina like a mother hen, holding the goblet of warmed wine for her to drink and chafing her hands to restore the circulation. He thought that she was probably in a certain state of shock. He did not know the details, of course, of the bargain she had made with his master, but if he knew Cesare the terms would be hard. He also knew that because of the state she was in they would be unable to move as quickly as he would like. Therefore their journey must be as secretive, as hidden as possible.

It took them more than Cesare Borgia's expected two weeks to return safely to Rome.

Piero had done his best but the Frenchman must

have had every man he commanded out searching for his wife. They eluded capture only by the skin of their teeth, more times than Piero would like to mention.

Valentina was so sick.

Every morning she was sick and Piero worried over her. It would be more than his life was worth if anything happened to her and he gentled her along the tortuous path towards their destination.

When they finally arrived in Rome, Cesare was appalled at her pallor and her thinness.

"Jesu! Piero what have you done to her? Why have you been so long?"

Valentina clung to him, so glad that the journey was over.

"We are lucky to be back safely, Monsignor. The Lion almost tore the countryside apart searching for her. 'Tis a good thing that you sent me. No-one else would have made it back here with the lady."

Valentina could hardly bear to think of him searching so fruitlessly for her. She should have left some sort of message for him. Explained why she had left.

Cesare was solicitous.

"Come, Valentina. Your chamber has been ready for days. You must rest and restore yourself."

His voice soothed her as he led her to the rooms prepared for her and she allowed herself to relax. Surely he would make few demands on her as long as she was not well. She would make the most of it while she could.

When she entered her chamber she stopped, stunned. Sumptuously adorned with every comfort and luxury any woman could desire, Valentina's quarters had had no expense spared on them and Cesare Borgia watched and waited for Valentina's reaction.

She turned and looked up at him, placing her hand on his breast. "It is too much, Monsignor..."

"Cesare."

"Aye, Cesare. It is too much. You spoil me."

He took her by the shoulders and his face was close to hers as it had been on that night when he had persuaded her onto the balcony in the Papal palazzo. He brushed back a stray wisp of hair and she forced herself not to flinch.

"Nothing is too much for my mistress, Valentina. I respect your honouring of your word. Few would have kept to their bargain and returned. You will not regret it."

His mouth touched hers in the briefest of kisses then he stood back and bowed with a flourish.

"I shall leave you now, Madonna. Antonino here will see to your slightest desire. You have only to ask."

The young man whom Cesare had named as Antonino, stepped forward as his lord left and Valentina acknowledged him with a faint smile.

"Something light to eat, Madonna?" Antonino indicated a tray which held a bowl of steaming broth and Valentina felt her stomach clench at the sight of it. She must eat, however. She must build up her strength to face whatever the future might hold.

After the first mouthful her appetite returned and the young man who waited on her beamed his approval as she finally wiped the bowl clean with the last morsel of bread.

"Will you bathe now, Madonna, or do you wish to get some sleep?"

"Sleep, Antonino. It seems a century since I last occupied a bed." – And shared it with Raoul.

She switched her mind away from the longing.

Antonino left her to slip out of her clothes and with a sigh she sank into the softness of the feather cushions, falling into unconsciousness almost, rather than sleep.

It was well after midnight when she awoke. She

panicked a little in the dark, sensing someone in the room with her. A candle was lit and although she recognised Cesare standing, a slight smile on his lips, looking at her, yet still she did not relax. She did not ask what he was doing there.

"Madonna. How do you feel? Recovered a little, I hope?"

Drawing the coverlets up to her breast, Valentina faced the consequences of her bargain with the Borgia. He came towards the bed, unfastening his doublet and letting it drop to the floor. The bed dipped to his weight and she found she could not look away from him. Those slumberous dark eyes were fascinating and she knew at once that he was not going to be told, no.

He reached out to caress her cheek and she could not help but draw back. He raised his brows.

"Do not disappoint me, sweet Florentine. You asked a high price and I gave it willingly, so the least you can do is return the compliment."

"I cannot." She whimpered the words, knowing that there was no escape, yet making the denial.

"Oh, but you can."

Suddenly he ceased playing and she found herself pinned back to the cushions, with his weight full over her protesting body. His mouth scored a burning trail down her throat and he pulled aside her shift so that his kisses could seek the softness of her breast.

Forcing herself to lie still, to keep to her word, Valentina found the tears coursing silently down her face and she repeated over and over in her mind. 'Forgive me. Raoul, forgive me.'

Cesare Borgia was no novice at arousing a woman and in spite of herself Valentina could not fight down her body's response to his expert caress.

He was not violent with her, choosing instead to rise to the challenge of coaxing pleasure from her unwilling body. Intoxicated by the sweet, tender skin beneath his fingers and lips, his passion built until he was almost blind with his desire and when he entered her he was forced to stop for a moment to struggle for control. She was shuddering with the boiling mix of emotion which gripped her and keeping her eyes tightly shut, she tried to pretend that this was not her husband's enemy in whose arms she lay, whose lovemaking was demanding an answer which her body was powerless to deny.

"Aah, sweet Valentina. Whatever happens from this moment, I shall always remember this. I shall never forget you, no matter on what paths the future may take us."

Then he could hold back no more and his cry of pleasure was a gasp of disbelief more than of victory.

When it was over, he pulled her into his arms and kissed her mouth with a passion that had barely subsided with his satisfaction.

"I do not think I shall tire of you so easily, my Valentina. These soft curves hold many a sweet hour of diversion yet."

She had no answer for him and he sighed as he left her bed so reluctantly.

"Duty calls. I do not know when I can return, but be assured that it will be as soon as possible."

When he had gone, Valentina lay staring into the darkness, her mind blank, her body still aching from the onslaught of his passion. Sleep claimed her like a thief in the night.

She did not awaken until the sun was high the following day. For several moments she lay where she was, summoning up the courage to face the day and what it might hold for her. With all the urgency and desperation of trying to save Raoul she had not had any real time to consider the consequences of the bargain she had made with Cesare Borgia.

To become his mistress was by no means the worst thing that could happen to a woman. Many famous women were not wives but mistresses and enjoyed a freedom and respect which some wives in not so happy marriages envied.

However, she longed for Raoul with all her soul and she knew that as long as she was away from him she would live in the depths of despair. The one thing she must not allow was to let Cesare see how she felt. She must live up to the letter of her bargain no matter how much she despised herself.

The sudden surge of nausea took her by surprise and she rolled to the edge of the bed retching noisily. The sweat started on her brow and her limbs shivered uncontrollably.

"Sweet Lord, I have been struck down with a plague for my sins. Please don't let me die! Dear Jesu' please don't let me die."

A brief knock heralded the arrival of Antonino, his brow creased with concern.

"Madonna. Let me help you. Here!"

He held a bowl for her as she strained to empty her stomach and when finally she collapsed back onto the bed, exhausted, he wiped her brow and face with a cool cloth.

"I shall fetch Monsignor's physician, Madonna. It is probably the strain of the travelling and it will be nothing serious, do not worry."

"No! Please, do not concern yourself. I am well enough and as you say, it is probably the strain of the travelling. Some food will help."

Not too sure, yet unwilling to worry his master, Antonino sighed and gave in to her. "Very well, Madonna. But if this persists, I must inform Monsignor."

All Valentina could do was nod, she was so weak. After Antonino had gone, she made an effort to pull herself together. She gave a little laugh. It was typical of fate really, she supposed, for Valentina had realised what it was that ailed her.

She carried the Lion's child.

What was she to do? For now, surely, all bargains were off. She was not prepared to risk her child here in the Vatican where he could be held as hostage against her husband. For the moment she must keep her own counsel. Her biggest problem would be in deceiving Antonino for he attended on her almost constantly. And then there was Cesare's passion. How to avoid that without seeming to go back on her word?

Sweet Mother of God. She needed help. Now more than ever.

Antonino entered with some food and Valentina made every effort to appear well and recovered from the sickness. He seemed satisfied for the moment and Valentina sat down to eat with a sense of determination. It was now vital that she build up her strength and make sure that she was as fit as possible to face whatever demands were to be made on her while she was here.

Cesare did not come to her that night.

Antonino brought her a message when he brought her her evening meal.

"Monsignor's deepest apologies, Madonna, but he has been called away from Rome for a few days. If you need anything at all, Monsignor has given me authority to look after you."

The relief was breathtaking. Almost the answer to her prayers.

"Thank you, Antonino. I am feeling much better and I think some fresh air would be beneficial tomorrow if that can be arranged."

"Most certainly. Eat well, Madonna."

She took his advice with meaning and he was most pleased to see the empty dishes when he came to clear away.

Alone in her room, Valentina tried the door out of curiosity. Outside was a guard. He came to attention.

"Madonna!"

"Oh! 'Tis nothing. I just thought to explore a little."

"Shall I fetch Messire Antonino?"

"No, no. No need. It can wait until morning."

She smiled and retreated into her room.

Leaning back against the door, Valentina cursed.

The window perhaps?

The height made her a little dizzy and she could have cried with frustration.

How long had Antonino said? A few days? She must find a way out of here by then.

It was scarcely light when Valentina rose the next morning. She was sick again but by the time Antonino came to her room she had regained her composure and made sure that all seemed well.

"There. You see, I was right. I feel well this morning. After I break my fast I should like to take a walk, if that is possible, Antonino."

"Most certainly, Madonna."

It was a beautiful day and if the circumstances had been different, Valentina would have thoroughly enjoyed herself. Antonino escorted her through the gardens of the Papal palace and she was most impressed with the beauty laid out for the pleasure of this Pope, Roderigo Borgia.

However, she was most closely watched.

Accompanied by not only Antonino, but also four guards. Cesare was most certainly taking no chances on losing this treasure he had coveted for so long.

For the next few days, the same routine was followed. She tried to suggest a walk out into the city of Rome but Antonino was smilingly firm.

"Too dangerous, Madonna. With things the way they are with the French. Most people seem to be leaving the city anyway for they are afraid that the French army will pass this way on its return to the north."

His words dismayed her. The French army was returning to France. He must count her dead or as good as. He would not want her anyway, now that she had given herself to his most implacable enemy. But he would certainly want his child.

What was she to do? Valentina racked her brains to no avail. She worked herself up into a state of despair.

The meetings with the states which were to make up the 'Holy League' bored Cesare to death. He could not get Valentina out of his mind. She seemed to have cast a spell on him that kept him in a state of perpetual arousal. He had thought that once he had had her then his desire would disappear or at least, abate. But it had him more on fire for her than ever.

"Monsignor?"

"What?" Cesare came to himself with a frown to concentrate on what was being said. Lodovico Sforza was holding forth. Cesare did not trust him. Cesare did not trust anyone, but the Sforza least of all. After all, it had been he who had invited the French into Italy in the first place. Still, they needed him. His skills as a noted condottiero would be invaluable against the French now that they had persuaded him to join them.

It was a great effort to push the sweet Florentine to the back of his mind and pay attention to what was going on but he had to do it for this meeting was vital to his plans to defeat the French.

Still she was there. Haunting him. He made up his mind to try and return to Rome sooner than he had intended, even if only for a brief visit.

In Naples, the Lion raged.

How had she eluded him? Why had she left?

Where was she?

The answer to the last question seemed obvious. She must be with the Borgia.

But why?

If she had wanted to leave him for that bastard

son of the Pope why had she raced against time to clear her husband's name? Why not just leave him to his fate?

He could not sleep. He could not eat. He walked the walls of the city like a ghost, despairing, impotent, furious.

Even Charles was sympathetic.

"She must have been forced into it, Raoul. If you had seen her begging me to have mercy on you..."

"Yes, Sire." If it had not been for that charge of treason she would be with him here now. Instead of with the Borgia. For that lecher could only have one use for her. He clenched his fists. The thought of Valentina in another man's arms, especially that man, brought on a killing rage which showed so obviously in his face that everyone avoided him. No-one would cross him. Some did not even have the nerve to speak to him.

There was only one thing the Lion could do.

CHAPTER XV

Charles finally decided to take the advice of Raoul de Baisleon. So many of his other commanders now supported the Lion that there was really little else he could do.

"We will leave a strong garrison here for I do not intend to give up my little kingdom so easily."

"They will be waiting for us, Sire. You realise that. They have finally stiffened their spines enough to get together and oppose us."

Charles spat. "That Borgia bastard and his Spanish allies. Even Sforza has turned against us. And it was he who begged us to come here in the first place."

"They still stand no chance against us. Their way of making war is all theory and posturing. I do not think any of them has killed in anger in their lives. A stiletto in the back is more their style."

Raoul's contempt was biting. He had made his own plans for the trip home and some of those plans concerned Cesare Borgia.

Valentina had not seen Cesare for almost a week. Her sickness had eased and her appetite had grown. She had put a little weight back on and her cheeks had regained their colour, her eyes their brightness. She avoided thinking of that night when she had been forced to make good her bargain with the Borgia for she knew that because of it any chance she might have had of ever returning to Raoul, had gone.

She tried to relax, although her future was so uncertain it would be better for her child if she tried not to worry too much. She decided to concentrate solely on the babe and what would be the best thing for him, for she was sure it would be a boy. An heir for Raoul.

She was still determined to escape and preferably before Cesare came back for she could not conceal her condition for ever. Her mind ferreted busily for ways and means.

"Antonino, I should like to write to my family in Florence. To let them know that I am well ."

"Certainly, Madonna." The manservant could not

see any harm in granting her request and so the writing materials were brought and Valentina set about composing the most difficult letter of her life. The only thing that worried her was that her letter might be read and so she had to be careful what she wrote.

In the end she merely told them where she was and that she was being well looked after. They were not to worry and she hoped that she might see them soon. She did not mention the child.

Little did she know what the reaction at the Palazzo Velucci would be.

Guido could not believe it.

Florence had not joined the Holy League, not trusting the son of the Pope, preferring to adhere to her alliance with the French. The priest, Savanarola exhorted the Florentines to stay loyal and stay loyal they did.

"My daughter, in the hands of the Borgias! What was her husband thinking of to allow such a thing? I have heard of carelessness, but to lose a wife in such a way. The man is mad!"

Bianca tried to calm him.

"Monsignor, we must think! We must think of some way to help. I am sure that she is not there willingly and I refuse to leave her in the hands of a poisoner, a murderer, a man who commits incest."

"How can we help? Are you mad also, woman? Do you want me to challenge Cesare Borgia perhaps?"

"Do not forget. Your daughter sends you a pension, Monsignor. What will happen to the money if she is no longer with the Frenchman?"

Bianca Velucci certainly knew her husband. He paled visibly at her words.

"You are right. We must contact Monsignor de Baisleon and let him know that... that..."

"Valentina."

"Yes. That Valentina has written to us. And something of her circumstances. He will know what to do."

Satisfied now, Guido stopped his pacing and gave orders for a letter to be written immediately and despatched by a courier on the fastest horses in his stables. Bianca still would not let it be, however.

"Perhaps you should ride to join the French..."

"Sweet Jesu' woman, do you want to kill me? Why should I do such a foolish thing?"

"You never know. The Frenchman may be so grateful to discover Valentina's whereabouts that he may be in a generous mood. A short journey and you may come out of this a richer man."

Guido took his wife's hands and kissed them impulsively. "Now I know why I married you. You are a genius. You are right. I shall leave immediately, adequately escorted of course. I shall have to hire some bravos, men who are not afraid to fight."

Raoul was astounded by the arrival of his father-in-law.

Guido was escorted into the presence of the Lion by a guard who had disarmed his hired bravos in seconds and with about as much trouble as taking a sugar tit from a baby.

Approaching Raoul, smiling, with his hands outstretched, Guido hailed him as a long lost son.

Raoul suffered an embrace for a scant second before standing back and holding up his hands.

"To what do I owe this pleasure, Monseigneur Velucci?"

Guido's face assumed an expression of woe.

"I came to offer my help. My daughter, your wife, in the hands of the enemy. My son, how did this happen..?"

"I knew it..!" Raoul felt the cold hand of fear grip him by the scruff of the neck. "Did you say, 'In the hands of the enemy'? How do you know where she is ? I have searched this damnable land until I am almost blind with looking. She is with the Borgia. I knew it. Why is she with him? What devilish bargain did she make to obtain my freedom?" The fear and the fury coursed through Raoul so that he almost cried out with the pain of it. He was so powerless. How could he, the Lion of France, be so powerless?

Even Guido Velucci could see that he had said something wrong, something very wrong indeed.

"Forgive me. We received a letter..." He fumbled in his purse. "Here. From... From... your wife." Damn his soul, he could never remember their names. There were too many of them.

Raoul snatched the crumpled piece of parchment from his father-in-law and read it avidly, despairingly.

Guido watched uncomfortably, shifting from foot to foot. He had not even been offered a glass of wine. The French certainly needed to learn some civilised manners.

"Fetch Lieutenant d'Imoges!"

The curt command sent guards scuttling.

"Monsignor?" Guido tried to attract his attention.

"What? Oh yes. Here!" Raoul unfastened his purse and tossed it to Velucci. Guido caught it deftly but protested.

"I did this for my daughter. I have travelled a long and dangerous road but I was sure that you would want to know about this."

Raoul paused. "I see. Then you wish to accompany us?"

"Accompany you? To where?"

"To Rome, of course." Raoul laughed almost exultantly. "Yes. To Rome." He crushed the parchment in his fist. "To the Borgia. And this time no-one will stop me taking full and exact revenge."

Charles' permission had to be sought.

Raoul was in no mood to be gainsaid.

"I cannot spare you. Particularly at this time. I leave half my men here so those who go with me are doubly valuable."

"I am sorry, Sire. I must do this. I cannot sit back and do nothing, knowing where she is. If you do not give me permission, then I go without it."

"I can have you arrested."

"Not without a fight this time."

The king huffed and puffed petulantly but was forced to give in.

"Very well. But I cannot do without you for long. Make sure you return as quickly as possible for we leave this land, reluctantly, within days."

"I shall meet you, Sire. I shall make sure that I

gather intelligence on the way so that we profit from this."

"Go then."

Raoul turned to leave.

"Take care. My compliments to your lady."

Raoul bowed and left, fierce exultation in his heart and the burning desire for revenge heating his blood.

Guido could not believe that he had got himself into this situation. It was all Bianca's fault. When he got back to Florence... No. If he got back to Florence, he would beat her silly.

The whole of the Lion's company set out to rescue their lady. The rest of the French army made ready to leave that seductive city of Naples and head for home. They left the day after Raoul de Baisleon.

To the north the Holy League massed to oppose them. Cesare Borgia was at their head. Much as he had tried, he had been unable to return to Valentina. If he had left at that point then the Alliance would not have stood for five minutes. Frustrated, he simmered with bad temper and they avoided upsetting him, afraid to encounter a knife in the back or the poisoner's cup. Cesare's reputation was growing.

The Pope had made himself scarce to his summer villa at Orvieto and most of the populace of Rome deemed it safer to do likewise and leave the city as the French approached.

Rome became almost a ghost town. Valentina, cloistered in her apartments and securely guarded, knew nothing of what was going forward. She was obsessed with the need to escape. She was slowly coming to the desperate conclusion, however, that it would be impossible.

CHAPTER XVI

"She is bound to be held in the Papal palace."

The murmured comment from Alain d'Imoges had his lord nodding his agreement.

The French were less than a day's ride from Rome and the council of war held in Raoul's tent was merely to discuss details of how they were to gain entrance to the Borgia's apartments.

The ideas and arguments harried back and forth without resolution until Raoul was almost driven mad with frustration.

Guido was becoming bored with all the fuss.

"I should have visited my daughter alone. At least I would know how she was, instead of all this fuss about how to get in here and how to get in there... What? What is wrong?"

The two Frenchmen, Raoul de Baisleon and

Alain d'Imoges were staring at Velucci with matching grins on their faces.

"The man is a genius."

"Why did we not think of this before?"

Guido frowned. They were all mad. Then he slowly realised what they were thinking.

"Oh no! You are mad. You cannot expect... You will not get away with it."

Raoul shrugged. "It is the only way. Rome seems to be half empty. We know that most of their soldiers are gathering far to the north, waiting for the main part of our own forces at the River Taro. It will be easy. We are simply your hired bravos, Monseigneur Velucci."

With a groan and a curse once more for Bianca, Guido could do nothing but go along with their plans.

Valentina thought constantly of Raoul. She wondered whether she would be allowed to visit Florence, to see her parents. She wondered what they had thought of her letter and whether she would receive a reply. She wondered whether Raoul had found consolation with another woman.

She had to get away. She thought to appeal to Antonino for help. But then if she did and she failed to gain his help he would be warned.

No. She must think of something else.

Rack her brains as she might, she could see no way out of the silken prison into which she had stepped.

It was so simple to enter Rome that Raoul was appalled. A band of twenty of Raoul's best men lay hidden, waiting for their lord's return, in the woods but he had deemed it best for just the three of them, Raoul, Alain and Guido Velucci, to attempt the actual rescue. He left two men in charge of their horses just outside the Janiculum gates.

They were not stopped nor challenged once. Guido trembled so much with fear that it was perhaps a good thing that no-one questioned them. He would have given everything away at the drop of a hat.

The citizens of Rome were frantic to escape, to be elsewhere when the French army passed. Raoul, Alain and Guido Velucci made their way towards the Vatican palace through almost empty streets.

"We need information. We need to know where he is keeping her. It is down to you, Monseigneur Velucci. Only you can carry this through now."

Guido Velucci looked into the eyes of the two warriors who faced him. He knew that they thought him a coward and a buffoon and stubbornness and pride came to his aid. Truly, Valentina was his daughter and although he was so dismissive of the girl children his wife had constantly presented him with, in his heart was still that fierce protective instinct which could not be denied.

He threw back his cloak with a flourish and strutted to the front of their little band.

"Signori. Follow on."

Alain and Raoul glanced at each other in surprise then followed behind the cocky Florentine who suddenly seemed to have donned the mantle of a condottiero.

The guards were few and nervous. Cesare had almost stripped Rome of soldiery in order to make sure that the Holy League would vastly outnumber the French.

Guido's lordly attitude impressed and they were soon being introduced to Antonino.

The young man bowed low. "Your pardon, Monsignor. I shall inform Madonna Valentina that you are here. She will, I am sure, be delighted to see you."

"Of course she will. I have made a long and difficult journey to get here. I have had to hire men to protect me and such men do not come cheap, believe me."

Raoul and Alain looked down, making sure their faces were in the shadow. Not the best time nor the best place to be discovered now.

Valentina was astounded when Antonino told her that her father had arrived to see her. At the same time, a surge of hope rose in her breast. Perhaps this was a chance. A chance to escape.

She had never hugged her father in her life but as Guido walked through the door of her chamber she almost knocked him off his feet with the enthusiasm of her welcome. Laughing and almost crying at the same time, she did not even notice the two heavily cloaked men who hovered in the doorway behind him.

Raoul was staggered at the wave of emotion which gripped him at the sight of his wife. His hands trembled as he hitched his sword round to a more easily accessible position and he was forced to calm himself so that the manservant crowding behind them did not suspect anything.

She is so thin, was his first thought and those eyes of hers were enormous, haunted and sad in spite of her being so glad to see her father. He wanted to snatch her into his arms and console her, wipe away that tormented expression that lay behind her great dark eyes.

Antonino was becoming concerned. The father was obviously genuine, Valentina's welcome had convinced him of that, but the two men who had accompanied the Florentine were, in his opinion, acting suspiciously. They should have waited outside.

"Signori. If you would wait outside, I shall send someone with refreshment."

The words were scarcely out of his mouth than he was pinned back against the wall by one of the men, a lethal stiletto at his throat.

"One sound and you're a dead man!" The hissed threat ensured Antonino's co-operation.

"Alain. Bind his arms and stop his mouth with something so that he cannot raise the alarm."

Valentina was watching the action over her father's shoulder with stunned amazement, her mouth open and her eyes like saucers. Before she knew it, Raoul had whirled back into her room with his sword drawn and had snatched up her cloak from a chair where she had discarded it after her walk only an hour since.

"Quickly! Don't just stand there staring. Move yourself, Madame!"

Shocked and disbelieving, yet with an insane desire to shriek with laughter, she did as she was told and with her father's arm about her shoulders, followed her lord and his lieutenant away from the place she had despaired of ever leaving.

Sparing a pitying glance for Antonino where he lay bound and gagged on the floor, she hoped he would not suffer too much from Cesare Borgia's wrath when he discovered she had fled, for he had been kind to her.

Raoul was fiercely jubilant. He had hold of Valentina tightly by the hand and even that contact made him feel invincible. He was not going to allow anything or anyone to stop him now. He had her and he was keeping her, one way or the other. His task was made easy by the fact that Cesare had kept his beautiful prisoner secret. To the casual observer she was now just any lady escorted by her husband or her father and a servant, out for some air and it would be a brave someone who would be prepared to question the likes of Raoul de Baisleon at the present time.

Valentina was dragged along, trying hard to keep up with the pace Raoul was setting and attempting to ignore the stitch in her side. Muffled in her cloak, it was impossible to tell her condition and she fought to stay calm. He had come for her! Through untold danger he had come for her. And whether it was to kill her or kiss her, she cared not as long as her eyes could dwell on his beloved features again. And he surely could not kill the mother of his child, however degraded he thought her! She felt that whispering touch of hysteria again but fought it. Everything must appear normal. No-one must guess that they were fugitives.

All went well until they reached the gates out of the city of Rome. So many people had fled before the advancing French army that the guard had now been doubled in an effort to stop the city becoming totally deserted.

Guido Velucci pushed to the front of the line of people waiting to leave the city, puffed up with bravado and a sense of his own importance.

"What is all this? Do Romans now regulate the movement of all the city states? As a Signor of Florence, I demand passage out of the city."

"Monsignor Velucci! What are you doing here?"

Guido stared, appalled, into the narrow eyed gaze of Piero del Aguila. Of all the men to meet he was probably the most dangerous. He stared back at Guido and then he looked past him to the bundled up shape of Valentina flanked by Raoul and Alain.

As recognition dawned, Piero stepped back and drew his sword. The mass of people waiting in line, scattered like leaves in the wind, leaving Piero with the guard at his back, facing the four fugitives.

Guido was terrified. Of all the men to meet, apart from the Borgia himself, this man del Aguila frightened him more than anyone. He stepped back so quickly, so frantically that he got in the way of Raoul and Alain who had drawn their own weapons and were making ready to defend themselves.

There were five guards with Piero but Piero del Aguila himself was probably worth two men. Raoul was wishing that he had brought that hidden band of his men closer in to Rome. He should have foreseen that they may be stopped at the gates. Whatever happened he would not be stopped, would not give her up. He would die first.

"Well, well. The Lion of France himself. Monsignor Cesare will be sorry to have missed you." Piero was going to enjoy this. And how great would be his reward when he presented his master with either the Lion as prisoner, or his dead body to display as a spur to the courage of the city states who faced the French.

"'Tis certain that your master will miss you when I have killed you." Raoul taunted him. He must concentrate on del Aguila. The others were nothing. Alain could probably see to them on his own. Once out of the gates on the other side of the Tiber, their men would be waiting with the horses. Just let him deal with this grinning bastard and they were away.

Valentina watched, horror-struck. She grabbed her father's arm fiercely. "Do something. Surely you are not going to stand there and gibber with fright while Monsignor and the lieutenant are slaughtered?"

"I am not a young man. I am no warrior. What do you expect?"

"Courage. I expect courage, father."

With a groan, Guido did his best. Having no weapon of his own, he dodged about and waited until Alain d'Imoges had dealt with one of the guards, then he scrabbled in on all fours and grabbed the dead man's fallen sword. He handled it gingerly. These things could be dangerous.

His moment came when Alain was fully occupied with two of the remaining guards and one man who had been wounded, got back on his feet and made the effort to attack the Frenchman from behind. With a shout, more to encourage himself than anything else, Guido swung the heavy sword and well nigh decapitated the unfortunate soldier. Blood sprayed everywhere. Guido was covered in it and he scrubbed at himself in disgust.

"Well done, Papa!" Valentina kissed him soundly on the cheek, then with a scream pushed him to one side. The man who faced him now was certainly not wounded and Guido found himself praying to all the saints to aid him as he circled around to avoid his opponent.

Luckily, the man was only young and he was totally inexperienced. Most of the able fighting men had been carried away by Cesare to oppose the French. Guido stood up to the clumsy blows aimed at him and then shutting his eyes he hurtled forward swinging his sword in front of him. A glancing strike found its mark and the young man fell to rise no more.

Guido was astounded.

Raoul was finding Piero a more than worthy adversary. The man knew all the tricks of someone of his dangerous calling and as they struck and whirled and circled around each other Raoul thanked his patron saint that he had kept himself fit during the months they had spent in Naples. The only thing bothering him was that time was against them. The alarm was sure to go up and then they would stand no chance against re-enforcements from the Papal palazzo.

Alain was still fighting hard. Guido's limited help had reduced the odds but it was still two against one.

A scream from Valentina made him turn his head. A fatal mistake. A ferocious, two-handed blow from one of his opponents felled him, blood pouring from his side. The man grinned in triumph and stepped forward to deliver the coup de grace. Alain fought to push himself upright. His fingers would not obey his command and his sword was grounded in the dirt. Sweat and blood mingled in the lieutenant's eyes and the darkness swooped in on him. His adversary raised his sword then he stopped suddenly and his eyes lost their focus before he fell forward almost on top of Alain d'Imoges.

Guido stood, trembling there, his sword dripping blood and his face white and shocked.

Raoul had gone down on one knee from a particularly vicious swipe from Piero's sword and it was that which had terrified Valentina so. With an immense effort, the Lion surged to his feet and with his war cry on his lips, hammered Piero to the ground. He turned to his lieutenant, sweat pouring from his brow, and shouted to Guido. "Help me! Help me here, if you value your own skin!"

Piero was trying to stand, trying to stop them and Valentina decided that she had stood helplessly by for long enough. With a shout she swung a foot at del Aguila, catching him full in the stomach. His breath whistled from his lungs and he fell forward, retching.

With Alain, bleeding heavily and almost unconscious, supported between them, Raoul and Guido made a bid for the open gates. Valentina caught up a sword from the ground and stood rear guard, backing away from the crowd whose courage was returning, who could scent a substantial reward if they captured these fugitives. Her shriek of defiance made them step back. They faced a wild-eyed madwoman wielding a man's sword and for a moment they hesitated and their chance was lost. Once through the gates Raoul was screaming at the top of his voice for his men and their horses.

They were waiting.

Horses thundered towards them and in the confusion of milling animals and whirling dust they made their escape. Within seconds they were all mounted, Alain tossed up behind one of the company, Valentina held tightly in Raoul's arms and as a belated surge of the crowd came through the gates after them, they left Rome in a cloud of dust.

CHAPTER XVII

They were not pursued. There was more on people's minds than chasing a runaway female, especially one whose protector was as able a swordsman as Raoul de Baisleon.

Piero del Aguila lay coughing up blood. He knew Cesare would have his life for allowing, not only the sweet Florentine to escape, but also her husband, the Lion of France. He must not be here when the Borgia returned. Even a lifetime of faithful service would not save him, for to the Borgia no-one was indispensable.

The fugitives headed for the safety of the French forces. They were more secure when once they were surrounded by the men of the Lion, but Alain was losing blood fast.

"We must stop, Monsignor." Valentina could see

him, hanging to one side, barely able to cling to the man before him. His life's blood ebbing, staining the horse's flanks.

Raoul stared grimly ahead, ignoring her plea.

"Monsignor, please!" Valentina grasped the neck of his doublet. "We must stop. Alain is bleeding to death!"

"I know this!" Savagely he answered her and the tears drowned her eyes. "We cannot stop yet. We are still too close to Rome."

"But he is dying!" She shook him and he swore. Slowing his horse, he raised his arm and his company drew to a halt.

Valentina struggled to be free of him, to slide down from the dancing warhorse and run to where Alain had finally fallen from behind the rider, to the ground.

"Pick him up. Into the trees. We must find some cover." The terse command galvanized his men into long practised action. Within moments they were concealed, with guards posted and the horses tethered close.

Alain clung grimly to life.

"Leave me, Monseigneur. I am slowing you down." He coughed, heaving for breath, increasing the flow of blood.

"Get away from him!" Valentina was crouching next to the young lieutenant who had had such care of her from the day of her marriage to the Lion of France.

As gently as she could she sliced open his doublet with the knife plucked from her father's belt. When the flesh was bared, she paled.

The ribs had been broken by the massive blow and the bloody froth bubbling at Alain's lips was tragic evidence that a lung was punctured. The bleeding from his side was nothing compared to the injuries inside. Injuries about which they could do nothing.

Valentina sat, lifting Alain's head gently into her lap, soothing back the sweat soaked dark hair. His blue eyes were clouded with pain and Valentina fought to control her weeping.

"Leave me, Monseigneur." The whisper was so weak, that Raoul bent close to hear him.

"I will not leave you! Let the Borgia send a thousand men. I will not leave you." The Lion gripped his friend's hand as though to stop him slipping away, but the fingers were cold and did not return his grasp.

"Madame?"

"I am here." She drooped her head to his, her hair

forming dark wings, a protective curtain about his face.

"Madame, take care of yourself. Take care of the child – and – do not forget me."

"Never! I shall never forget, Alain... Alain!"

His eyes lost their light. The terrible bubbling breath stopped. With a despairing cry Valentina clasped him to her, rocking him against her breast as she would her babe.

Raoul felt a band of steel tighten about his chest and he cursed the name of Cesare Borgia, wishing him in hell and swearing revenge for the only man who had been his true and trusted friend.

Guido wept unashamedly. In spite of the danger and all his cowardly blustering, he had truly believed that they would all come out of it in one piece. The death of the young lieutenant was a shock, a tragedy he found difficult to accept. He muttered a soft prayer and bowed his head.

Raoul finally stood and put his hands on Valentina's shoulders trying to urge her to her feet. She shook him off.

"No! Not yet. Please Monsignor."

"We can do nothing more. We need to meet up with Charles – then at least I can fight. I can seek the Borgia in the ranks of the 'Holy League'." He said the name with scorn.

"We cannot leave him. I will not leave him."

"He must be buried. This heat..."

"I do not care. I cannot leave him. Please."

"Very well." He sighed. "He goes with us."

It seemed to be the only way to coax her away and as she allowed herself to be raised from the ground, gently resting Alain's head back in the grass, Raoul gave orders for his friend to be wrapped up in their cloaks. A litter was quickly constructed and he was bound securely to be carried on the litter between two horses.

Valentina watched, her father's arm about her shoulders, desperately trying to stem the flow of her tears. When finally they were ready, Raoul stepped close to his wife. Her face was red and swollen with weeping and gently he brought up his hand to caress her cheek.

"Do you ride with me?"

Too racked with grief to hear the appeal in his voice, Valentina gestured dazedly.

"I will not bother you, Monsignor. I will slow you down. I can ride alone."

His hand dropped to his side and his brief, "As you will." was muffled as he turned away to order his men to make ready.

Belatedly, Valentina held out her own hand, realising that she had said or done the wrong thing, but it was too late. He had swung to his horse and taken the lead, leaving her to be lifted to her horse by her father.

"A touch ungracious, daughter." Guido's gruff comment stung and the tears started again, weakly, causing her father to shrug and shake his head at the vagaries of women.

The company of the Lion travelled steadily for another day until finally they were eating the dust of the tail end of the French army. The baggage train stretched for miles and Raoul thought that Charles must have stripped Naples of everything of value that was transportable. There was a laden mule for every two men and the slow pace of travel did not bode well for their chances of getting out of Italy unscathed.

Turning his horse, Raoul cantered back to Valentina.

"How are you faring, Madame?"

She took a deep breath. She had been doing a lot of thinking during the long hours of their headlong journey to catch up with the army.

"I do not think that I can sit my horse for much longer on my own, Monsignor. Perhaps I overestimated my own strength." She could not meet his eyes, looking down hard at her hands holding the reins in a grip which whitened her knuckles.

He stared at her as the meaning of her words sank in then in a single movement he reached across and lifted her bodily to sit before him. A nervous laugh squeaked from her throat. Guido nodded approvingly, drooping a wink that only Valentina saw.

"Is that better?"

Her mouth was close, so close to the strong brown column of his throat and it was a fight for her not to simply purse her lips and press a kiss to the pulse she saw beating there.

"Yes, Monsignor. Much better."

When she thought how she had longed for him during those lonely days spent in the luxurious apartments fitted out for her by Cesare Borgia. The miracle was, that her desperate ploy in obtaining those incriminating letters from Cesare, had saved him. Had saved him so that he could come and rescue her from the consequences of her rash bargain with the son of the Pope.

Raoul felt her soft breath on his neck and his arms tightened about her. He had her back and nothing would wrest her from him again.

By the time they reached the van of the army, they had been regaled with all the news concerning the whereabouts of the army of the League and Cesare Borgia.

"The camp followers know everything before the king and his commanders. They are invaluable as spies."

It was very difficult for Raoul to talk normally when the desirous weight of Valentina in his arms was playing havoc with the demands of his body. Still, he could scarcely throw her down on the grass and take her. Not after all she had been through and certainly not in front of the whole of the French army.

Also, the death of Alain was playing on his mind. It was hard to come to terms with the loss of his friend. As a warrior he should be well used to it but he cursed the day that Charles had been invited so temptingly to take the kingdom of Naples. The only good thing to come out of it so far, was Valentina.

He sat his warhorse, his tender burden before him, a grim figure looking neither to left nor right, ignoring the the thronging crowds of whores and thieves who clung to the skirts of the French army like excrement to a sheep's tail.

They watched him, him and his lady and their

escort; some with envy, some with admiration and one, one with black, bitter hatred. One who spat in their wake as they passed then dodged back into the anonymous crowd before she could be recognised.

Charles was very glad to see Raoul de Baisleon. Raoul was brief in his tale of the rescue and made his point quickly.

"We need to bury my lieutenant, Sire. With your permission."

"We are moving slowly enough, God knows. My condolences. I know he was your friend and loyal friends are hard to find. Go. See to it."

"Thank you, Sire."

It was Guido Velucci who found the perfect place for Alain to rest.

"There is a small monastery, not too far from here, on land that once belonged to Florence before this rapacious Pope came to his throne. My family have been benefactors there for a few generations. He will not seem to be amongst strangers."

The place was peaceful. Far from the main travel route and surrounded by poplar trees, it was not a fashionable monastery but when Alain was finally laid to rest, Raoul made sure that it was certainly much richer than it had been. "Take care of my friend. I may pass this way again."

They returned to the army in sombre mood. Valentina made it to the tent which had been prepared for her but as she leaned forward to dismount, her ordeal caught up with her.

Raoul was there to gather her into his arms as she fell.

"Louis. Fetch a physician."

He ducked into the tent with his precious bundle and Guido stood for a moment, wondering what to do. Tact came to his rescue and he made himself comfortable by the smouldering campfire, rehearsing the stories he would tell when her reached home.

Inside the gloomy tent they were alone for the first time in what seemed like centuries to Valentina. Her head was swimming and she felt sick. Raoul felt her brow and swore. It took him only moments to strip her down to her shift. The little maid, Deodora, had been left behind in Naples for she had found herself a man and had begged to be allowed to stay. Raoul found himself, therefore, in the role of nursemaid, a task which he surely did not find onerous.

"I should not have let you ride. I should have made you travel in a litter."

"We did not have time for such niceties,

Monsignor. Do not worry about me. I am strong."

"I know this." He smiled and her heart felt as if it would burst with love for him. He took a tendril of her hair, wild and loose where it had come free from its tight coils, winding it around his finger and wondering at its silkiness.

"Why did you go to the Borgia?"

She had known he would ask the question and she had dreaded it. What could she say? That Cesare owed her a favour because she had not raised the alarm at his escape? That would make her a traitor. She took refuge in weakness. Closing her eyes and turning away her head, she pretended faintness and what could he do? He could not force her to answer. The reckoning would come but she wanted to be ready. If she could but delay his questioning until the signs of the child were more obvious then perhaps he would take a softer view of what she had done.

A disturbance at the entrance to her quarters distracted Raoul. The king's own physician had arrived to attend the Lady de Baisleon and her husband stood back to watch anxiously as she was examined with calm thoroughness.

When he had finished he kept them waiting. As physician to King Charles, this man liked to foster his image of importance.

"All seems well." Finally he spoke. "What the lady needs is rest and nourishment." He looked sternly at Raoul de Baisleon. "Is there nowhere where she can stay instead of being dragged along in the tail of the army? If fighting starts, as I am sure it will, this is no place for a woman who is four months or more with child."

"With..? What did you say?" Raoul felt as if a great hand was squeezing his heart and he struggled for the words.

The physician looked at the Lion sternly, unimpressed by his reputation.

"I said that the tail of an army is no place for a woman four months or more with child." He repeated his words slowly and loudly as though to an idiot. Raoul was not looking at him.

Valentina trembled.

Raoul fell to his knees beside her and drew her close to his breast. She tried to avoid his eyes but he put his fingers under her chin and forced her to look up at him.

"When were you going to tell me? When my son was red and squalling in the midwife's hands or when he was ready to wield his own sword?"

Valentina put her hand to her brow.

"You may leave us." Raoul spoke the words to the physician without even turning to look around. The man huffed his disapproval but deemed it best to be diplomatic.

"I had no chance. There seemed to be no good moment."

He could feel her trembling and he set his lips gently to her hair. A soft laugh escaped him. "There seemed to be no good moment? And what if I had not come for you? How would you have gone on then?"

"I would have thought of something."

"Surely you would, my sweet Valentina, you would have thought of something. Sprouting wings to fly perhaps. Well you are here and safe now and do not ever try to leave me again."

"No, Monsignor."

He laughed again, wishing that he could be convinced. Still, perhaps the child would slow her down.

Guido had hovered anxiously while the physician had been inside the tent and when the man emerged, affronted, he had waylaid him.

The news astounded him. And he agreed with the physician. His daughter could not possibly stay with the army in her condition. She must return to

Florence with him.

"No. She stays with me."

Raoul forestalled Guido's offer.

"But Monsignor, apart from anything else, she will be much safer in Florence where her mother can look after her."

To Guido, it seemed the only sensible thing to do. But then Raoul was not inclined to think straight where Valentina was concerned. Holy Cross! He had only just got her back!

He looked at her lying there, her dark hair spread out now across the cushions, her face pale and tired, eyes swollen with all the weeping for Alain.

"What..? What is your wish, Madame? Do you stay with me and face the danger or do you go back with your father?"

There was a moment of silence and he thought that he should not have put the onus on her after all she had been through but then her answer brought a thrill of elation.

"Monsignor, I stay. As long as it does not endanger the child I carry, I stay with you."

Guido cast up his eyes in exasperation. The physician tutted. Guido had persuaded the man to re-enter the tent with him so that he had some support.

Raoul took hold of his wife's hand, unable to stop touching her, trying to convince himself that she was really here with him again.

"At least get a woman who knows how to care for her. Surely the wife of one of your men? And make sure she rides a wagon. We are moving slowly enough with all this baggage." The physician shook his head. "Of course, I shall take care of her. The king was most explicit in his orders, but still she needs a woman."

"I shall find her someone."

"Very well. Make sure she is clean, whoever you find. Most important."

When the physician had gone, Guido made a further protest.

"Please, Monsignor de Baisleon, consider again. She will be very safe at Palazzo Velucci and as soon as you reach France and are safely installed, I can make sure that she joins you as soon as possible."

"No!" They said it almost together and Raoul glanced down at her. Valentina had made up her mind. She would enjoy his attention while she may for when the time came for questions and she was forced to answer, why he could find that he did not want her with him after all.

CHAPTER XVIII

Camille de Brieur was filthy dirty. She considered the state of her blackened and broken finger nails and the torn remnants of a once magnificent gown, and cursed for the millionth time the name of Raoul de Baisleon and his wife and that lisping idiot of a king who had led them all into such a doomed adventure.

And now she, the hitherto spoiled and pampered darling of every man at the French court, was hiding in fear of death or imprisonment, amongst the camp followers of the army.

She had watched him bring her back.

Cesare Borgia had also fallen so much under the spell of that Florentine bitch that he had traded incriminating documents for the pleasure of the use of her body, documents which had resulted in

Etienne de Brieur's downfall and her own ignominious flight into this vile whoredom and the precarious existence of a camp follower.

"Want some?"

Camille turned to accept the offer of some food from Eloise, one of the whores who had befriended her when first she had sought refuge in the huge and sprawling melting pot of the French baggage train.

"'Tis no good you just watching him. You can't do anything about it. Best just set your sights on one of the sergeants, a decent man who'll look after you.."

Camille shuddered at the thought of 'a decent man to look after her.' No. Revenge was a dish best eaten cold and her dish was cooling rapidly. Now the bitch was back and pregnant too, by all accounts. Well that was even better.

Raoul worried over her. When she had had some rest and hot food, her colour had returned and she did not feel so sickly. But still he worried.

Guido had made up his mind to depart for Florence.

"Bianca will be wondering what has happened to me. She will surely want news of Valentina..." Not much chance of him forgetting this daughter's name again in a hurry. "...and the babe. Send a messenger when you are within reach of us and I shall try and bring Bianca for a visit. After all it may be the last chance we will have of seeing you again."

Valentina embraced him tightly. Her view of him had changed. He was still cowardly, she knew, but she could no longer condemn him for that.

"Take care, father."

"I shall send a strong escort with you. They can scout the way ahead and bring us back information also. Fare well."

They waved until Guido Velucci and his escort had dwindled to dots in the distance then Raoul put his arm about Valentina's shoulders to guide her back to her tent.

"Monsignor, I am not an invalid."

She laughed up at him and his arm tightened about her, turning her into a full embrace. He stared down at her, his golden gaze devouring her features.

"Now, Valentina, I have you safe and you will not escape me so easily again."

The fiery head descended, his arms gathered her close and his kiss started that fire in her blood which banished her weakness. She clung to him with all her strength, as though she was afraid she would lose him.

"Valentina, Valentina. Why did you take such a risk? Why did you go to the Borgia?"

Was she never to evade that question? She knew that he could never let it rest, that he needed to know how she had acquired such evidence to clear his name. What had she given in return for such help?

Her hands gripped his shoulders and she stared straight into that puzzled, almost hurt gaze and spoke so softly that he had to bend to hear her.

"Monsignor, what I did, I did for love of you. I thought never to see you again whichever way things turned out. Either I would be unable to obtain the proof I needed and you would die, or I had to give myself in return for that proof. In that case, how could you ever want me again?"

Her last words held such an appeal, such a burning question, that he could scarcely take breath to answer. Those words of his to Camille de Brieur, it seemed so long ago now, returned to haunt him. How could he take a wife in whose fidelity he could not trust? The thought of Cesare Borgia's body covering hers, the thought of his lips kissing her, almost drove him to the edge of insanity.

Yet Valentina had done it for him.

She had risked her life, risked everything for him.

For she could have been killed, tortured, imprisoned. How could he condemn her for that?

He could not. He would not.

"You ask how could I ever want you again? My sweet love, how could I ever not want you?"

"You still can say that you love me, after I have lain with another man?"

He closed his eyes on that stab of pain.

"I say that if love is needing the touch of someone so much that it aches. If love is a pain which can only be eased by the presence of that someone, then I love, Valentina. I love you."

Oh God! She had thought never to see him again. Never to hear him say those words, 'I love you,' again. She reached up with trembling fingers to touch his cheek. With a smothered curse he pulled her to him once more, his lips descending on hers in a kind of desperate seeking which she had never known in him.

"When I discovered you had gone I was lost. I knew what you had done. I could not understand why you had left me after going through so much for me. Do not leave me again!"

"I swear I shall stay with you always. You will never be rid of me!"

His laugh rang out and then he laid his hand to

her stomach.

"You must take care of our son. Rest. 'Tis a long journey home."

"As long as I have you to care for me. That is all I need."

Her words sobered him.

"A woman. We need a woman. Who will know of a suitable woman?"

Both their thoughts turned to Alain and it was so hard to face the fact that he was no longer with them. No longer there to organise them.

"I shall ask amongst the sergeants. There is sure to be a camp follower who may be suitable. A respectable woman, perhaps, who has fallen on hard times or who has chosen to follow a man she loves."

Eloise watched Camille's face as she told her that she had been asked to look after the wife of the Lion of France.

"'Tis a judgement. My chance for revenge. Will you help me?"

Eloise was not certain. There was something about Camille which frightened her. Still, there might be something in it for her, some reward.

The look on Camille's face was so intense, so determined. Finally, Eloise could do nothing else but nod.

"Very well. I shall let you know how things go. But I am not doing this, risking my life, for nothing."

A sardonic laugh was her answer.

"Do not worry. I shall repay you, in full measure."

Valentina carefully weighed up the woman who stood before her.

Her name was Eloise. A Frenchwoman who had followed her man through all the campaign to Naples, she had lost two children with disease and had a huge-eyed youngster clinging to her skirts. Thumb in mouth, the child watched as the lady searched for a sweet meat to give him. He sucked happily as his mother answered the lady's questions.

Clean enough, the woman spoke well for herself and Valentina made up her mind.

"Very well. I require a maid. Nothing too demanding here. Just to help with my bathing and dressing and to fetch my meals. Is that to your liking?"

As long as she could feed the child, Eloise would do just about anything. But she did not say that. Just nodded.

The French army moved ponderously northward.

Cesare Borgia made his plans. He did indeed miss that right arm of his, Piero del Aguila, but it was as well that the man had made himself scarce for how could Cesare support someone who had let him down so badly? In the insane rage which had gripped him at the discovery that Valentina had gone, Cesare might have murdered his own father.

And the sweet Florentine?

Well, perhaps it was best to have sweet memories. He would most certainly have tired of her eventually.

Wouldn't he?

Valentina was growing heavier with the child she carried. Each night Raoul gathered her to him in bed. They had not made love since her return, although desire for her was hot within him and the touch and scent of her made his pulses race.

"Is the woman to your satisfaction?"

"Aye. The child is so sweet. He fascinates me."

"Soon you will have your own to fascinate you."

"And to fascinate you, I hope, Monsignor."

"You fascinate me."

His fingers trailed her body leaving a shiver of wanting in their wake.

"Tell me again of Baisleon."

She tried to distract him. He grinned at her ploy

and would not be distracted.

"It will not hurt."

"No. It will not hurt."

He savoured the taste of her flesh. She rolled over and his fingers caressed her back, biting gently at her shoulders and neck. The insinuating stroking of her thighs made her gasp and whimper, tipping back her head and offering her mouth for his kiss.

Valentina was astounded at the breadth of his shoulders and she savoured the curve of muscle, the hardness of the flesh beneath her fingers. Closing her eyes and breathing in the scent of his body she almost floated away on the intensity of her desire for this man.

Raoul cupped her buttocks and raised her to lie atop him. Disbelieving, she felt him enter her, slowly, almost tentatively. Tipping back her head she gave herself up to sensation, each stroke of his love arousing shivers of pleasure throughout her body. That sensitive, desirous core of her being was touched at each push of his hips, eliciting sighs of ecstasy which only increased his passion.

Desperately, he tried to go steadily, not to be too rough with her, but it took every ounce of iron control he possessed to be gentle with her. He watched her face, her closed eyes, the tip of her tongue which wet her lips, and the shake of her head as she threw back her hair in her pleasure.

That ache, that burning ache which flared deep within her, made her cry out, cry out his name then she collapsed towards him, her kisses raining down on his face, his eyelids, his mouth.

Fiercely, he kissed her, cupping her face with his hard, warm hands and groaning against her mouth as he too reached the heaven which beckoned.

Weak and shaking, they lay in each other's arms and laughter bubbled forth.

"I have ridden many a strange steed in the past, Monsignor, but never one which groaned so at the spur."

"Insolent hussy. I can see that you will need beating every so often to keep you in your place."

They smiled at each other in the dark and snuggled close then they slept, Valentina's leg flung across the legs of her husband, relaxed and happy.

In the darkness, Camille watched, a half smile on her lips. The guard caught a shadow in the night and moved forward to challenge whoever it was lurking there, but when he looked again there was no-one.

CHAPTER XIX

"It may be too dangerous. Savanarola has changed his tune. The French are now the enemy. I wish the lunatic would make up his mind so that we can all decide who to hate!"

Guido Velucci had returned safely to Florence and the arms of Bianca. He had regaled them all with the tales of his exploits, how he had rescued, almost single-handed, his daughter Valentina and how grateful the Lion had been for his help.

The French were now approaching Florence once more and Bianca had expressed her desire to see her daughter.

"But, Monsignor, you promised."

Her husband had seemed to have a new lease of life since his return and Bianca was enjoying a new found spice to her marriage.

Guido cast his eyes up to heaven. He was beginning to be sorry that he had made himself out to be such a hero. Perhaps if he could send a messenger to Raoul de Baisleon and he would provide an escort?

Raoul could scarce believe it.

"A messenger from your father. It seems that your priest has turned against us and it has become dangerous to be allied to the French. However, your mother is desperate to see you and Velucci asks for an escort to see him safely to our camp."

Valentina could not hold back the giggles. Finally even Raoul could see the funny side of the situation and the soldiers within earshot smiled at the sounds of merriment issuing from the camp of the Lion.

The French were camped between Arezzo and Siena and their sentries were constantly besieged by flurrying skirmishes with troops from the Holy League.

"We shall wait until we are nearer Florence. We must pass almost by the walls of the city and so it should be easy enough to arrange for your mother to visit. That is if she is allowed out of the city."

"Thank you, Monsignor. I shall be most grateful to see my mother before we disappear into France, for it may be a long time until a visit so far can be arranged."

"And you will be fully occupied at Baisleon, looking after me and our son."

That smile of his did its usual strange things to her stomach.

"And what if it is a daughter? Will you be as devastated as my father was? What if I bear you nothing but girl children, will you put me aside?"

"Never!" He pulled her into his arms. "I shall keep you to amuse me. The infidel, it is said, has women whom he keeps purely for his pleasure. I would keep you purely for my pleasure."

"And I would get nothing from it at all. I would pass my days in sadness and weeping."

He pressed his brow to hers and dropped a kiss on the tip of her nose.

"Well, I am sorry for that. But you will have to bear it."

They smiled into each other's eyes.

The one watching them was almost sick. She still considered her revenge, still worried over what would be the most satisfying way to destroy them. Eloise had said that the woman was about six months gone. Camille had had it in mind to just kill Valentina, but really that was far too simple, far too easy. No. She wanted them to suffer as much as possible and at the back of her mind was a glimmer of an idea. It would mean biding her time, staying out of the way and watching. Just watching for the moment.

It was June before they saw the walls of Florence and the River Arno was merely a trickle of water winding its encirclement of the city.

The priest, Savanarola, who had hailed the French as saviours only six months before, now called down the wrath of God upon them, calling them traitors and forbidding Florentines to welcome them in any way.

Guido was exasperated. Bianca was determined to visit Valentina and so in the dark of the night they slipped out of the city with only six men to protect them and made their way to the French encampment. They were almost captured and marched away as spies at one point but the name of the Lion of France was as powerful as ever.

Eventually, Valentina found herself folded into her mother's ample embrace. Raoul found himself saddled with Guido Velucci.

They stayed overnight, talking and eating and boasting until dawn when the massive army started out once more and it was almost noon before Bianca and Guido had waved their daughter and her husband out of sight. They stood together watching as company after company of men marched past. The great guns, pulled by teams of horses impressed Guido immensely.

"This Holy League will stand no chance against that sort of artillery in spite of outnumbering the French. She will reach her home safely, do not worry."

Bianca smiled and her gaze wandered to watch a small group of camp followers who were arguing over a ride on one of the guns. Bianca frowned briefly as she saw a blonde whore eventually win the battle by slipping down her shoulder ties and making the officer in charge of the gun an offer he could obviously not refuse.

There was something about the blonde woman which did not fit, somehow. It was the way she carried herself. Her arrogance. Then Guido plucked at Bianca's sleeve and she forgot the incident as she followed her husband back towards Florence.

Steadily the French forged towards home.

The heavily laden mules slowed them down and it was July before they approached the passes of the Appenines.

There the huge army of the Holy League awaited

them, on the banks of the River Taro.

There had been frantic to-ing and fro-ing for several days. The French were totally confident, in spite of being so heavily out-numbered, and indeed their men, so professional, trained to kill, trained to face the enemy without ever breaking rank, were far superior to the ranks of mercenaries which opposed them.

Raoul still desperately missed Alain d'Imoges. He had no-one, now, on whom he could rely to look after his wife. No-one whom he could trust to send with her while he, himself, went into battle.

In the night, she knew he worried.

"Raoul, I shall be safe. You must not think of me when you are fighting for that way lies danger. You must concentrate your mind solely on the battle, solely on the enemy."

"I know, you are right. But I could not bear to lose you again. I would want to die, for life would hold no pleasure for me."

She felt the blood drain from her face at his words and she tried again to reassure him.

"I have Eloise and that hulking great sergeant of hers to protect me. It would be a brave warrior to face that duo."

She succeeded in wringing a laugh from him and

he considered her words thoughtfully.

"You are right again. The man is a good fighter and he seems to have some sort of brain. I shall put him in charge of your escort and see how he fares. If he does well, I shall promote him. The child who trails her looks better of late."

The small boy, son of Eloise and her man, had stolen Valentina's heart and she made sure that there was always food to tempt his appetite. He had put on weight and had lisped one or two unintelligible words, causing a fuss and praise which confused yet delighted him.

Eloise was grudgingly grateful yet seemed sometimes to discourage Valentina's attentions to her son. Valentina shrugged although she was a little hurt by her maid's attitude.

Slowly the two armies grew closer together.

Raoul spent much time closeted with Charles and with the other commanders, discussing their line of battle. Tired and dispirited, the French just wanted to go home. If they could just overcome the hotch potch of forces which faced them, then their way was clear for there would be no-one else who could stop them.

The summer heat shimmered over the combatants and the men sweated in their armour.

Valentina had armed her lord that morning as she had armed him on the morning of the attack on Monte di San Giovanni and he had given his final instructions to Eloise's man, Arnaud.

"Stay with the baggage. They continue to head northward while we engage the enemy here. It will be safe enough and they would not attack a band of women, these chivalrous play actors. They are about to find out what war is all about."

Raoul still harboured a hope that somewhere out in that horde before them, Cesare Borgia waited. The banner of the Borgia bull was hard to miss and the banner of the Lion would seek to engage him should he find him.

Valentina stood to wish him fare well.

He took her by the shoulders and drew her to him.

"Fear not my love. Once we have broken the enemy here, the road home is free and clear. Our son will be born on his own lands."

Valentina lifted her chin and smiled into the lazy lion's eyes.

"I am not afraid, Monsignor. But, please. Take care. Come safely back to us."

His head bent swiftly and his kiss was sweet on her mouth then she was left to watch as the commanders moved to their troops and readied themselves for this last effort.

They had been well briefed. The artillery bore the main responsibility for softening up the enemy and Valentina flinched as the bombardment began.

"Come, Madame."

Arnaud took her arm and helped her to mount the wagon which already held Eloise and her son.

"Do not worry, Madame. They will not defeat us. Your lord will be safe."

It was a surprise to hear Eloise volunteer an opinion and Valentina smiled and then turned her attention to the child who was trying to climb upon her knee.

Steadily the baggage wagons forged forward. Valentina could see her friend, Etoile d'Erpignan, together with two of the other ladies of the court, just a few wagons in front of her. She had been so occupied with Raoul that she had not mixed with the rest of the court ladies and she made up her mind to remedy that once they were all safely away.

Behind them the tail of the camp followers stretched as far as the eye could see and Eloise, her maid, was staring grimly back towards them. Valentina turned to see what she was staring at but could notice nothing unusual and so she concentrated on keeping her seat on the bumping wagon and forgot about it.

The sounds of battle, the thud of the guns, seemed to echo around the surrounding mountains and it was only when the wagons began to haul to a halt that Valentina realised that the battle seemed somehow to have got in front of them. Confusion ensued. Screams and shouts of alarm jerked Valentina to her feet and she could see Etoile d'Erpignan struggling with a heavily armed man who was trying to drag her from the wagon.

"Arnaud! Quickly! The enemy are in front of us. Take Eloise and the boy. These wagons are their target and we must leave them."

The sergeant did not argue and within seconds he had his son in front of him and his woman clinging behind. One of his men vacated his saddle and boosted Valentina up in his place then leaped to pillion behind another man.

At seven months gone, almost, Valentina felt heavy and clumsy on the horse and cursed the attackers who were seeming to roll around them like an angry tide. Still she was determined not be captured and torn again from her man. Arnaud was laying about him with a will and the enemy fell back slightly allowing them a passage through the press of bodies. Then as they thought they had won through, Arnaud's horse went down, stumbling over discarded loot, and Eloise and her child were thrown to the ground. Arnaud could do nothing. His cries of pain confused Eloise. Trapped beneath his horse he was an easy target for the Italians who were attacking them.

"Hold! Wait, wait. Arnaud needs help."

Valentina screamed at the rest of her escort and reluctantly they pulled back to group around their lady. They all knew that should anything happen to her because of them, they were dead men.

"Eloise! Quickly, here to me." She shouted to the woman who was trying to drag her man free of the struggling horse. Finally the panic stricken animal surged to its feet, leaving Arnaud on the ground, his leg broken.

The French soldiers formed a ring around Valentina and two of them caught hold of their sergeant and in spite of his screams, threw him bodily across the pommel of a saddle. The child was sitting, crying, in the midst of it all and Valentina heaved herself off her horse to gather him into her arms. The problem was, that then she could not remount. Not with that great belly of hers hampering her every movement. Her horse was almost cantering around her in a circle and she did not know how she kept hold of the reins and the child both.

"Steady. Steady. Whoa now." She tried to calm the animal but it was useless and so she struggled forward with the boy clutched to her and her fingers fastened in a death grip on the reins of her horse. Her men were confused, unsure of what to do, whether to stop and fight off the Italians while they got their lady aboard her horse again, or just to keep moving in a tight group away from the conflict.

Alain d'Imoges had never been so desperately needed as now, but then Eloise was there, taking her child from Valentina and helping to hold the horse and boost her mistress up, struggling like a fresh landed fish, into the saddle once more. She handed up her son and then took Valentina's arm to be pulled up behind her.

Valentina laughed exultantly and kicked her horse forward, with her escort streaming around her. They surged away from the fighting and made for the protection of a small wood skirting the hillside before them.

From their vantage point they watched as the baggage train was plundered and the mules driven away towards the Italian forces, leaving behind a trail of destruction. Valentina wondered how Etoile d'Erpignon had fared, sorry that she could not have helped but knowing that they, themselves, had only escaped by the skin of their teeth.

Eloise watched, expressionless. Her man was alive as were her son and herself, only by the grace of the Lady de Baisleon.

CHAPTER XX

The thud of the guns had stopped.

Dead and dying lay everywhere and the French cut through the Italian forces like a hot knife through butter. The troops of the Holy League had never seen anything like it, never seen anything so bloody and ferocious in all the campaigning of the old condottiere. Greatly outnumbered as they were, still the French forged onward towards the north leaving behind a trail of screaming, wounded men for the camp followers to rob and cut up with their knives and axes.

Camille de Brieur took full advantage of the situation to steal anything she could carry. Most of the other camp followers avoided her. There was some sort of menacing quality about her which frightened them. So unthreatened, unmolested, she enriched herself and when she left the battle field, she was as bloody as any of the warriors who had fought that day.

The Lion of France had searched in vain for the Borgia bull. The Holy League forces which faced them were so vast and consisted of so many noble houses allied together that it was almost impossible to seek out one man amongst so many. Besides, Raoul was so intent on getting through this battle and returning to his wife, that his desire for revenge had really dwindled. What did it matter? Valentina was his and she carried his child. The Borgia was most certainly the loser in the bargain he had made.

It was as they were leaving behind the main part of the battlefield that news started to filter through that the baggage train had been attacked. He could scarcely believe it. Here he had been smugly congratulating himself on the way things had turned out and now this.

Frantically, he hacked his way through what remained of the opposing troops, his heart in his mouth at the thought that he might have lost her again, and cursing himself for being so careless, so self-satisfied.

The things the camp followers were doing to the injured Italians made him sick to his stomach but his concern for his wife overrode all other feelings and so he rode right past Camille de Brieur without even seeing her.

What remained of the baggage and belongings was being hauled wearily along in the wake of the army once more and Raoul spent precious time questioning those who had survived.

It was Etoile d'Erpignan who gave him hope. Sporting a huge black eye, nevertheless she was irrepressible and shouted up to him.

"Do not tell me that you have mislaid your lady again, Monseigneur de Baisleon."

"Have you seen her?"

"Certainement! She did not wait to be attacked but took her company towards the woods. She should be safe enough."

"My thanks." Floated over his shoulder as he pressed his horse towards the direction she indicated.

She was sitting as if on an outing, a cup in her hands in the shade of the trees. His men were in a tight circle about her, and she turned from offering the child a drink and watched him throw himself from his horse, with a smile on her lips.

"Well, Monsignor, you took your time!"

The tired but teasing voice brought a leap of joy

to the heart of the Lion of France. He swept her into his arms, uncaring of his watching men and kissed her almost with exasperation.

"Can you not stay where I put you, Madame? I can see that I will have to chain you down when we reach home."

She laughed. "Tis a good thing I did not stay where you put me. And I carry considerable weight already, Monsignor and certain to get heavier."

"You are not hurt?"

"I am not hurt. But, please, do not ask me to get on another horse. The child will be born a centaur if we continue like this."

"I shall steal a wagon from the king for you to ride, my love."

"And the fighting?"

Raoul shrugged. "They stood no chance against us. They have always played at war and are not ruthless enough. The way home is now open for no-one will dare to try and stop us."

A groan from Arnaud distracted him.

"What happened?"

The men were binding Arnaud's broken leg and Eloise was hovering over him in concern.

"We realised that the baggage was being attacked and tried to get away. The sergeant's horse went down and landed on him. He will have to be carried."

He thought briefly of the fate of the wounded on the battlefield and nodded.

"Of course. Two wagons, then, from the king."

They laughed again together, then Raoul gave his orders and his men spread out around them while he and Valentina walked hand in hand to catch up with the tortuously slow moving main army.

They did not camp until after darkness had fallen, for they had wanted to get as far away as possible from what was left of the League army.

By the time Valentina was safely and warmly installed in her quarters she was totally exhausted. Eloise fussed over her and then stood iron-faced as Raoul ducked through the opening of the tent to see how she was.

"Madame needs rest and quiet. She will not miss you tonight, Monsignor."

Raoul was stunned by the woman's nerve.

"'Tis alright, Eloise. Monsignor is not too demanding a husband."

Valentina struggled to keep her face straight as Raoul could not hide his indignation.

"Charles has called one of his councils. 'Tis only

to be expected, I suppose, but I shall not disturb you if it goes on too late."

"Can he not rest? He must think you are all made of stone. I care not the lateness of the hour, but do not leave me to sleep alone."

Ignoring Eloise, Raoul pulled Valentina gently against his chest and placed his lips against her hair.

"As you wish. I care not to sleep in the cold in any case."

She looked up, loving it when he teased her. They had grown so close that they could almost read each other's minds, knowing when the other thought something was funny or tragic.

He stroked back her hair and cupped her face in his sword-roughened hands.

"At this pace we shall only just reach Baisleon in time for the babe to be born. Ahead lies some dangerous travelling. Perhaps your father was right. I should have left you in Florence until you had had the child. It would have been safer."

"No. I told you. I stay with you. No-one will part us again. I love you."

Eloise watched as the Lion kissed Valentina then she gathered up her child and left the tent, silently.

Camille chortled over her horde of looted

treasure. Soon she would have no need to prostitute herself. A few more battles such as this at Fornovo and she would be a rich woman in her own right. She had had a little time after Etienne had been arrested to grab some jewellery, but nothing like what she had possessed and the thought of all she had lost drove her to the point of insanity.

She really should not be hanging around the French army like this. She should leave, get as far away as possible and make a new life for herself, somewhere where no-one was likely to recognise her. Revenge, however, drove her on. Her hatred of Valentina was such that she would risk everything, even her life, to wreak revenge on the wife of Raoul de Baisleon.

A sound in the dark made her quickly conceal what she had been gloating over and when she turned, it was to see Eloise returning with the sleeping child in her arms.

"He returned safely, then. I saw him galloping to save his true love, but he did not see me."

"If I was you, I would leave it be. I have told you. Find yourself a man and forget those two. You only risk your life or freedom for a moment of triumph."

Camille grasped Eloise's arm so tightly that the woman winced.

"So. Do you turn on me now? Will you betray me to the Lion?"

Eloise shook her off easily.

"You're a fool! 'Tis only I puts up with you. I betray no-one but try and talk some sense into you. Leave here. You are a beautiful woman and well bred, anyone with half an eye can see that. You could easily have a very good life still. Heed my words and leave them alone."

Camille was wary of alienating Eloise. The woman had looked after her well, protecting her from the worst that camp life had to offer. God knows why she had done it. Camille could not afford to fall out with her.

"When will she whelp, do you think?"

"She must be careful. It is her first and they often come early. If she starts while we are travelling the mountain passes, she could have problems, in spite of that popinjay who thinks that he knows everything, just because he looks after the king."

Charles' physician and Eloise had not hit it off and it was only that Valentina had insisted on having her that she had been engaged as maid.

"So, it could be any time?"

"Aye. This careering around on horseback will not do her any good. She should have gone with her family and stayed in Florence until she had had the babe. But she will not leave him."

"Huh! Probably afraid that his fancy will wander and she will be left to fend for herself."

Eloise laughed.

"No chance of that! He has eyes for no-one else, I'll say that for him. He loves her."

The woman may as well have stuck a dagger in Camille's heart. It was certainly not that she had ever loved Raoul de Baisleon herself, but that he loved Valentina somehow was an agony that Camille could scarcely bear. She knew that her husband, Etienne had loved her but she had been unable to return his feelings. He had bored her. She envied this love that could face any danger. This love that could sacrifice anything for their lover.

Well, they would soon know what sacrifice meant.

The child in Eloise's arms murmured in his sleep and Camille hunched away.

"I hope the brat is not going to keep us awake all night again."

Eloise did not answer, simply stood up and walked away into the darkness leaving Camille alone and staring after her.

CHAPTER XXI

Finally, the French started up into the mountain passes. The pace was even slower than it had been because of the difficult terrain and the wagons became stuck in narrow ways where there was nothing else to do but unload them and tip them over into the valleys below.

The only benefit of the mountains was the cooler air and Valentina breathed deeply of it to try and restore some of her energy. She was finding it a torture to place one foot in front of the other for her wagon had gone the way of many of the others and she could not bestride a horse in her condition.

Eloise struggled beside her. At least Arnaud was back on his feet, although still lame and he gave his son a back ride to the child's delight.

"What is his name? You have not said."

Eloise glanced at Valentina and smiled. "He is called Charles, Madame. A small joke on my part."

"He is looking well, at least."

"In most thanks to you, Madame."

"Nonsense! He is so lovable, anyone would wish to spoil him."

Valentina stumbled and Eloise caught her, helping her along the way. The tall, gaunt maid was very strong and Valentina was most glad of her care.

The French army was now a tatterdemalion band who struggled, mauled and weary towards home. Louis, Raoul's page was no longer the carefree lad he had been. He had grown ridiculously out of his clothes and Valentina had finally had to insist that he take some of those things which had belonged to Alain d'Imoges.

"Madame, I cannot." Close to tears, the boy shook his head.

"You must. Louis, no-one could have loved Alain more than I and I know that he would have wanted you to be warm, would have wanted you to have use of those things of his which are left."

Finally he gave way to her insistence. He had to or finish the march naked.

Charles, the king, had given up calling those

interminable councils of his. Although he had lost most of his treasure at the Battle of Fornovo and had also lost Naples to the alliance of the Holy League, he still considered himself the victor of the conflict. The Sforzas of Milan had been detached from the alliance so that the latter part of the French withdrawal from Italy, at least, lacked the unending skirmishes which had worn them down so.

The nearer they drew to France, the more jubilant Raoul became. Valentina spent each night in his arms although he grumbled good naturedly and teased her about the space she was taking.

All seemed fair for their homecoming. The ladies of the court, all of them much thinner than they had been, were in high spirits in spite of the conditions in which they were living. The camps at night started to take on an almost carnival atmosphere. Songs in the light of the flickering flames of the campfires had a romantic air about them and there was many a sweet assignation when the flames of the fires had died. Etoile d'Erpignan, of course, was the instigator of most of the fun. She was a born party giver.

"When we reach home, do not lose touch, Valentina. You must visit. Although I do not intend to waste much time on Monsignor's estates. I much prefer court life to mouldering away in the countryside. When the court is at Avignon you must come and we shall have such fun."

Valentina would just be glad to reach civilisation. She was weary and heavy and she wondered sometimes how Raoul found anything attractive about her. She felt like a cow waiting to calf. Her breasts had swollen and she had no suitable clothing with her that would be comfortable for a pregnant woman. She did not know how much longer she could endure the travelling.

Charles' physician was gloomy.

"Monseigneur de Baisleon, you should have taken my advice and left Madame with her family in Florence. She is nearing her time and we have still to negotiate the high passes. We shall be safe in Savoy. Why do you not find a convent and leave her until she is delivered?"

Raoul did not know what to do. He was worried about Valentina and he wished that, indeed, he had listened to advice and sent her back with her father.

"Very well." He made his decision. "As soon as we cross into Savoy, I shall make sure we find a suitable place where we can stay. I will not leave her."

As it was, the choice was taken from him.

They had camped for the night just outside the town of Novara and Valentina had declined an invitation from Etoile d'Erpignan to join them in visiting the town which was under the rule of the Sforzas.

"To think, a chance to purchase some new clothes and to bathe and be clean. Are you quite sure?"

Valentina nodded and waved at her friend as the laughing, excited group left. All Valentina wanted was to sleep. She wished she could sleep for a year and she refused the food which Eloise had prepared for her. The woman frowned, concerned. Here, outside a friendly town, they could relax a little and Eloise had heated some water for her mistress to wash. Barely able to stay upright, Valentina allowed herself to be attended to like a child then she lay down on the cushions and watched in the torchlight as Eloise used the water to bath her Charles.

Somehow, she could not get comfortable and in spite of the fact that she was so weary, sleep was elusive. She rolled over from one side to the other, seeking a position where she did not feel like a bloated cow and Eloise paused in her bathing of her son to stare at the lady as she sighed and wriggled.

"Lie back, Madame. Let me see."

As Eloise gently examined her, Valentina was hit by the first pain. It took her by surprise and she was left gasping for air as it receded.

"Louis! Louis!" The maid's shout brought the gangling youth running. "Fetch Monseigneur. Quickly!"

It took a while to locate Raoul for he was at his duties checking his sentries and while they waited, Valentina was racked by the pains and sweat soaked her clothes. Between spasms, Eloise made her drink a brew of raspberry leaves which she had been gathering daily as they had travelled. They grew in abundance up here in the north and August was the best time to gather them.

When Raoul finally arrived he was trailed by Charles' physician.

"Stand back. Stand back, woman. Let me see."

"Nothing to see. Nothing you can do that I cannot." Eloise stood up to him, almost as tall as him and most threatening.

Another cry from Valentina sent Raoul to his knees beside her and Eloise was forced to stand back and allow the physician through.

"Hot water."

"All ready." The maid's tone was sardonic.

"I cannot see that there will be a problem. Madame seems to be managing things well herself."

"As I said."

"You are sure?" Raoul could not believe that this was his Valentina. She was sweating, her face contorting with the pains. Her eyes were fixed on the folds of the tent above her. She was young and strong but the strain of the constant travelling, the threat of attack had taken its toll. Her vision blurred and the next spasm of pain was such agony that she fancied that she was being ripped apart.

Vaguely she heard their voices, heard their murmuring.

Raoul. He was there with her. She felt his touch, his kiss against her temple, his soft encouragement and she whimpered his name. The whimper turned to a cry of protest as the pains surged through her again and Raoul felt the panic rise. Surely she should not be in so much pain? Could they not do something?

As Valentina heaved and sobbed in her agonies, Raoul could stand it no longer. His face white and his eyes deadly, he suddenly whirled on the physician and grabbed him around the neck almost throttling him. "Do something! She cannot bear this. If she dies, so do you."

The physician choked, trying desperately to release the Lion's fingers from his throat.

"Monseigneur! The babe is here!" Eloise's cry saved the man's life. Casting his victim to one side, Raoul turned back to Valentina.

"Almost there, Madame. Just a little more effort." Eloise encouraged Valentina.

Raoul held her hand, uncaring of her nails drawing blood as she heaved in her labour.

Finally she screamed one last, defiant time and fell back, exhausted, panting for breath.

There was a suspended moment of silence and then a thin squeak, a splutter and a wail.

Eloise held him up triumphantly.

"Here he is, Monseigneur. A fine boy."

The 'fine boy' wailed again and Eloise dried him off quickly and wrapped him up to lay him at his mother's breast.

Valentina was floating. Weak, shaky, she struggled to sit up, to hold her son. Raoul put his arms about her and held her cradled against his chest, watching as she cooed over the baby, as she put him to her breast to suck.

The fuzz on the babe's head glinted in the torch light and Valentina smiled and glanced up at Raoul. The glint was echoed there and she felt her heart swell with her love for them both.

The physician slid unobtrusively out of the tent, deeming it wiser to return to where he might be more appreciated.

The boy, Charles, crept close to watch as Valentina suckled her son and Eloise finished cleaning away the soiled linen, washed her hands then bent to pick up Charles.

"I shall make you some broth, Madame."

They scarcely heard her, so wrapped up were they in their son and each other. Eloise allowed a smile to lighten her usually sombre features then left them to go out to the fire, her son holding on to her fingers.

"Have you thought of a name?"

Surprise made Valentina look up. It was usual for a first born son to have a family name but as her eyes met his, that golden glance so dark that it seemed black, the same name was on both their lips.

"Alain. I should like to call him Alain."

His smile was sad as he remembered his friend and Valentina reached up to pull down his head and offer her mouth for his kiss. Out in the darkness the glow of the fire illuminated the face of her maid. Eloise ladled some broth into a bowl, ready to take it through to the lady.

The figure who suddenly hunched next to her aroused alarm. Eloise looked around to see if they were observed before hissing her warning to Camille de Brieur.

"You are a fool! If they catch you here it is the end for you."

"She is delivered of her whelp?"

"Aye. A boy."

"I heard her screaming."

There was silence for a moment then Eloise stood up.

"I must take her some food. You must go."

Camille pulled her cloak about her and drifted back into the night.

Eloise waited until she was sure Camille had gone and then she handed little Charles a morsel of bread dipped in the broth before going back to the tent with Valentina's food.

Raoul was leaning back against the cushions with Valentina propped up on his chest. The babe, Alain, heir to the Lion of France, guzzled greedily, his hands waving aimlessly in the air.

Eloise brought the broth to Valentina and took the baby from her while she ate. He was asleep immediately, his wrinkled face content.

"Eloise." Valentina took a breath between

mouthful of broth.

"Yes, Madame."

"My thanks."

"And mine." Raoul dropped a kiss to Valentina and then came to watch his son as he slept.

"You will have more substantial thanks when we reach Baisleon."

She could not look at him. Her struggle was inside. She wanted to warn these two of Camille and her implacable hatred, yet there was a pity for Camille herself, an understanding of how she felt, which kept her still silent.

"It is nothing Monseigneur. My duty."

Her abruptness surprised Raoul but he was so absorbed in his own happiness that he merely shrugged it aside.

Valentina could not finish her broth. She lay back and her eyelids closed. She drifted into sleep.

Camille was laughing softly to herself and muttering. The child. What sweet revenge that would be.

CHAPTER XXII

The army was moving on without them.

They were safe enough in the lands ruled by the Sforza and it was not far now to home. The company of the Lion was such that it would be a brave or a lunatic adversary who would attack them.

Charles' physician had been persuaded to return and examine Valentina and the babe and he had pronounced them both healthy.

King Charles himself, had come to see the Lion's son and heir.

"I will stand Godfather for the child. One of the few good things to come out of this campaign."

Charles had lost almost all of the treasure he had accrued in Naples, at the battle of Fornovo, along with many French heirlooms and a book containing the bound portraits of his mistresses. He seemed to mourn the loss of that more than the fabled sword of Charlemagne, which had also been taken.

Camille was furious. How could she stay behind if the army left? Her warped mind ferreted back and forth in her frustration. What could she do?

The town of Novara lay below and it seemed that the time had come for her to kiss the army goodbye.

She talked her gun captain into escorting her as far as the gates of the town. He did not want her to go.

"Stay with me. I treat you well." He was uncomfortable, finding it difficult to express what he felt.

Camille laughed. "What? Stay with you, a gun captain, and follow you on each campaign, or be left behind with a litter of brats?"

The captain's face hardened. "As you will." He was not one to beg. He remounted his horse and cantered back towards his guns, not looking round, leaving Camille de Brieur to take a breath and advance on the town of Novara.

Etoile d'Erpignan and her friends had squeezed in a final trip to the town before they were forced to take to the road again and as they and their escort clattered out of the gates, Camille was forced to jump aside, turning her face away from the dust and stones thrown up by the horses' hooves.

Etoile glanced down at the cowering figure and frowned, but then they were past and away up into the hills and she had no opportunity to analyse why the woman had seemed familiar.

Eloise was glad to see the last of the army, which took a full day to finally disappear into the hills. She had not seen Camille to bid her farewell and she was sorry for that. Still, she supposed that brawny gun captain would be looking after her and it was just as well that she would be out of the way of Raoul de Baisleon and his family. Perhaps Camille would now have to forget about her revenge.

Valentina had recovered well from the birth and she was glad to be able to move lightly about once more instead of lumbering gracelessly.

Raoul was a man in a daze. He could not stay away from his wife and son, watching as she tended to him and played with him.

"He is like you." Her voice was tender.

"Yet his eyes are dark like yours." His fingers caressed her cheek and she leaned her head back against his shoulder. She felt safe, secure, loved. Their happiness was so total, so complete and the journey home to Baisleon would not take so long.

Valentina would soon able to bestride a horse and without the hampering tail which dragged at the main army, they would make faster time.

The company of the Lion had cheered the child when Raoul had held him high for his men to see, until the hills around echoed to their acclaim.

"Alain, Charles, Raoul de Baisleon, son of the Lion."

He had not murmured, the babe, as the roars and cheers rose deafeningly, drawing the attention of even the people of Novara.

Camille de Brieur had found herself a protector. It had not taken her long. She had made an effort to tidy herself up, washing the long blonde hair and purchasing some decent clothing with some of the gold she had looted from the battlefield. Taking a room at a small hostelry, she passed herself off as the widow of a gun captain from the French army. Most of the Novarese had been sympathetic. Cesare Borgia was not looked upon with favour in these parts and since the ruling family of Milan had pulled out of their bargain with the Holy League and that mastermind of intrigue, the Borgia, his name was muttered with contempt.

One of the local merchants, a man who had made his riches from trade with Venice, had made it his business to get to know this comely young widow as soon as he could.

At first, Camille was not sure that she needed him. Then as he displayed more of his wealth in order to impress her, she decided that he would do to while away the time until she was ready to move against Valentina and her son.

From what she had learned from local gossip, it seemed that she had a week or so in which to formulate a plan before the Lion made ready to move out with his lady and his heir, towards home. She was going to need some help and she cast about for some suitable bravos to hire. Men who knew how to keep their mouths shut. Men who were prepared to turn their hands to anything in return for gold.

There were always mercenaries for hire and she did not have to look far to find the kind of men she sought. They stood before her in the room above the inn which she had made her home for the moment.

"I need men who will cavil at nothing. Men I can trust. I can pay well for the right kind of service."

"I can give you the right kind of service, Madonna." The foremost of the six men before her leered at her and her features hardened.

"Get out!"

He stared at her, uncomprehending.

"I said, get out." Her blue eyes glinted like chips of ice and although for a moment he faced up to her, she was so dangerous as she stood there. She oozed such threat, although she was only a woman alone, that he backed down. With a bow and no further argument he left.

After that she had no trouble with the other men and when she had finished she was most satisfied with her hirelings. A more cut-throat band it would be hard to find.

The only problem now lay in reaching Valentina and her son. It might be best to wait until they took to the road again. With the men she had hired, she would be able to safely follow at a distance and await her opportunity. She wanted to see Eloise, to speak to her and enlist her aid, although she was somewhat doubtful of where the maid's loyalty might now lie. How was it that that Florentine bitch could charm everybody into supporting her? Even Cesare Borgia, that manipulative creature, had been enthralled by her, to the point of betraying his spies in the French camp and causing Camille's present misfortune. Perhaps the woman was a witch.

A shudder of superstitious fear went through her briefly then her hatred blotted out all else and she turned her mind back to her plans.

The leader of her small group of mercenaries was closeted with her for an hour. When he emerged it was to tell off a man to keep watch in the hills, to spy on the Lion's encampment and report back on any movement there.

CHAPTER XXIII

Raoul watched her as she slept. The babe lay in a crib beside the bed, fist in mouth, deeply asleep also.

He found himself amazed at his good fortune. He remembered the first time he had seen her, laughing, leaning out from the balcony, frightening his horse. Then when he had spotted her in the gloom of the old minstrel's gallery at Palazzo Velucci, spying on the festivities below. He laughed softly.

The dark waves of her hair were spread about her and he gently lifted a few strands away from her face. There was an ache in his throat which he found difficult to swallow. When he thought he had lost her to the Borgia he had almost gone insane. Now he had his son to love also and he could scarcely wait to reach Baisleon, to show her his home and his lands.

Softly she stirred and turned towards him, seeking his warmth, the strength of his arms and he held her close, his lips tender at her brow.

He had never thought to feel this way about another human being. He had lost his parents when he was only a boy and there was a vague memory of his mother's softness and care. After they had died he had grown up very quickly. The power of his position had been envied by many and as he had grown to manhood and proved his prowess as a warrior, he had come to trust no-one. Only Alain d'Imoges had been allowed to get close to him, to become his friend. And him he had lost.

So now there was the three of them. And he meant to protect these two with his own life if necessary.

Valentina opened her eyes on the remnants of her dream. It had not been a good dream for it had held a threat and it was the reason she had turned to him in her sleep, certain that he could chase away the demons.

He tightened his arms about her. It seemed a lifetime since they had last made love. And it was only a week since she had been whimpering in labour. He could not take her yet, although his need was great. Never had he gone so long without a woman, but if he could not have this woman, then he wanted no other.

Trying to distract himself he thought of a visit to Novara, perhaps the next day. He would like to buy something for her, something to celebrate the birth of their son.

"Come with me tomorrow. We will ride down to Novara and spend the day there. The town will give us a good welcome, I am sure." Whispering so that he did not wake the babe, he bent close, his breath feathering her ear. Valentina shivered and tipped back her head, coaxing him into the kiss for she desired him as much as he desired her. A groan and he crushed her to him, fighting for control, knowing that it was too soon.

His son awoke and spluttered a sudden demand for attention and for food. Valentina could not ignore that age old appeal and reluctantly she pushed at Raoul. A curse was quickly stifled and he let her go to attend to Alain.

"I will not be long. Just some air." If he did not get out he would give in to his body's clamouring and that was not how he wanted it to be.

The cold air hit him like a slap in the face and he took several deep breaths before being drawn to the glow of the fire.

His sentries were alert. The nearest man dropped his pike to en garde until he recognised his seigneur and Raoul nodded his satisfaction.

Eloise materialised next to him. Charles had been restless in the night and she had been tending to him. She smiled at the harrowed look on the Lion's face.

"Not much longer, Monseigneur."

He hunched a shoulder at her.

"I do not know what you mean."

"Nay, Monseigneur. I mean nothing."

Was she laughing at him?

She was amazed that he had not sought relief with another, a whore even. No-one would have blamed him. All men did it. But not this one.

"Salt water will heal your lady quickly and then – why then you may start all over again."

He really did not want to discuss this.

"How is Arnaud?"

"Still a little lame. But sound enough to do his duty." Eloise defended her man.

"I do not doubt it. And your son?"

"A little colic. 'Tis nothing."

Raoul knew she had lost two children and that this child was, perhaps, a worry to her.

"I shall be looking for a good man at Baisleon to train up the young men we left behind as boys."

Was it a promise she heard in his words?

"Arnaud is a good man."

"Aye. I think so too."

They smiled at each other in mutual accord.

"I think I will check the camp. Tell Madame if she asks."

"Certainly, Monseigneur."

She watched him leave and was glad that Arnaud served one such as the Lion. They were most fortunate.

The broth she had prepared for little Charles was hot enough now and Eloise bent over the fire to pour some of the broth into a bowl.

When she straightened, the bowl slipped from her fingers and fell to the ground, unheeded.

"What are you doing here? You should have left with the army."

"So! You turn on me also? I thought I could count on your help. I thought you understood how I felt."

Eloise's glance slid past Camille de Brieur to where the sentries lay slumped on the ground, their throats cut. Carefully, she forced herself to bend and pick up the fallen dish. She must not allow Camille to read her feelings.

"I do understand. I have felt the desire for revenge myself. But I would not put myself at such needless risk to achieve it."

"Hah! You do not understand at all! And I do not have time to persuade you."

She gestured to the men who were with her and they moved towards the tent where Valentina suckled her son.

"No!" Eloise threw herself at Camille. "You will not harm her, nor the child! Aux armes! To me! Arnaud!"

Screaming for help, Eloise grabbed at Camille, swinging her around by the neck of her cloak and throwing her to the ground.

Her cries for help brought Arnaud at the run and Valentina to the entrance of her tent, the babe in her arms.

"Get back, Madame! Go in." Eloise screamed her warning then fell in a heap as Camille grabbed at her ankles and pulled the maid down on top of her.

Eloise was taller than Camille and strong, but Camille was insanely determined to achieve her revenge and the two women rolled over and over in the dirt, each attempting to gain the advantage over the other.

Arnaud had swung into battle with Camille's

men, roaring the Lion's battle cry and rousing the camp to the defence of the Lady de Baisleon and her son.

September was here and the air at night was cooler. Raoul sniffed appreciatively and looked up to the stars, diamonds in the night, exhilarating, dwarfing, wondrous. As he walked the perimeter of his camp, he suddenly felt that Alain was at his shoulder, as he had so often been in battle and some of the sadness, the sense of loss, left him.

The last sentry on the road above Novara was uneasy. He thought that he had caught a flicker of light in the hills above, but as he had stared into the darkness trying to pinpoint that faint spark, he told himself that he must have been mistaken. When his seigneur appeared suddenly behind him, the man nearly had a fit.

Raoul frowned. Why was the man so jumpy? They should be safe enough here in Sforza territory.

"Is all well?"

A fraction of a hesitation, then, "Aye, Monseigneur."

Raoul noticed the hesitation and he felt that tightening of his muscles, that premonition of danger which had saved his life in battle many times.

Taking the sentry by the shoulder, Raoul kept his voice low.

"What have you seen?"

The man did not want to make a fool of himself, yet he knew that his seigneur would rather that, than be taken by an enemy.

"It may be nothing, Monseigneur."

"Tell me."

"Over that way." He nodded to where he had seen that elusive elf light. "Some sort of light, or a fire. I know not, Monseigneur." He sighed. "'Tis probably naught."

Raoul knew that the man was wrong. Something, or someone was out there. Every nerve in his body told him this.

"Keep good watch. I shall send more men to watch with you. You have done well."

Walking back towards his quarters, Raoul de Baisleon felt a prickling between his shoulder blades, as though he was being watched and also there was fear, fear for his wife and his son. He had been too complacent. They would not be safe until they were home in France, in Baisleon.

The shouts and clash of steel hammered at his senses so suddenly and shockingly that several seconds went by before he could react.

Then Raoul de Baisleon started to run.

His heart pounded so fiercely that he sobbed for breath and he did not realise that he was yelling insanely for his men. He wore no sword, fool that he was, yet he hurtled into the midst of that madness, that confusion of whirling swords and contorted faces with only his courage and his determination to make sure that his wife and son came to no harm to protect him.

Camille had broken free of Eloise. A knee in the maid's midriff had driven the breath from her and she fell to one side, gasping and retching. As Camille staggered forward, heading for Valentina, Eloise frantically reached out, scrabbling at her ankles. A backward kick connected with her jaw and sent Eloise crashing into blackness.

Valentina cowered in the tent, clutching Alain to her breast. There was no way out through the fighting men around the tent yet how could she stay there and wait for Camille de Brieur and her men to come and kill them?

Snatching up the coverings of Alain's crib, she

wrapped the babe securely and rolled him out of sight beneath the hangings of the bed. She prayed that he would sleep on, fully fed and satisfied until the attackers had been dealt with.

As she straightened up she met the triumphant and vindictive gaze of Camille de Brieur.

Camille laughed. "So! The little Florentine! We meet again at last."

Her eyes roved the tent.

"And where is your whelp?"

Valentina made no answer, yet she cast about her for a weapon. Raoul's sword hung there in its scabbard and she looked away from it quickly.

"He is safe." Carefully she edged towards that sword.

"Well he will not be safe for long. You and the brat – Yes. I shall leave the Lion your dead bodies as my gift." A giggle escaped her, the blue eyes shining with delight and Valentina noticed then the knife.

A long-bladed, deadly stiletto, glinted in Camille's fist and she brought it up suddenly, on a level with Valentina's face.

The shouting outside intensified and Camille's face changed an instant before she launched herself across the intervening space between herself and

Valentina.

As Camille made her move, Valentina dived for her husband's sword, crying out as clawing fingers fastened in her hair, pulling her back, preventing her from reaching the precious weapon.

Cold steel was against her skin and Valentina's thoughts were only of what would happen to her son without his mother then she felt the warm flow of blood soaking into her hair, down between her breasts and into her mouth and eyes.

She sobbed her despair, unaware of any pain except that of leaving her son and Raoul. She fell forward onto her hands and knees beneath the weight of Camille and was crushed to the ground.

CHAPTER XXIV

The heat had returned, briefly, in an Indian summer as the company of the Lion crossed the passes of the Alps and returned home onto French soil.

Raoul sat his horse impassively, thinking of that hurried burial in the hills outside Novara and regretting that things had come to pass in such a tragic way. His one goal now was to reach Baisleon with his son and as the thought of the babe came into his mind, he glanced back towards the woman who carried the hiccuping bundle, heir to the Lion of France.

The wagons carrying the baggage and the women trundled slowly along, more slowly than he would have wished and his eyes searched the horizon, still not secure, although there should be little danger to such a company as theirs now that they were in France.

"One more week, Monseigneur, and we cross into our own lands."

Arnaud was gleeful, looking forward to reaching home with Eloise and Charles and anticipating the honours which had been promised him by his lord.

"How is Eloise?"

"She fares well, Monseigneur, thank you."

"When will the child be due?"

"Towards the New Year, Monseigneur."

"I am glad for you, Arnaud. And you know that you will go well rewarded for what she did."

"She was only glad that she was in time. If the woman had found the child..."

Raoul's face tightened.

"How I could have been so careless..."

"We all should have known. The woman was mad and Eloise felt that she was responsible for harbouring her during the march from Naples."

"Ah well. 'Tis all in the past now." He sighed heavily. "Another hour. Then we seek a place to camp."

"Yes, Monseigneur."

It was fully dark by the time the camp was settled and Raoul had checked and double checked the sentries. He knew that he was being paranoid, perhaps, but after what had happened at Novara he could not take any chances.

The camp fire was leaping hungrily at the carcasses which were the result of a good day's hunting and the smell of the roasting meat made his stomach growl in anticipation. Eloise tested the meat and nodded her head in satisfaction.

"Just about ready, Monseigneur. We are all hungry tonight."

The wail of the baby rose thinly on the cool night air and maid and master smiled at the sound. The cry stopped abruptly and Raoul could not stay away any longer.

He ducked through the entrance of the tent then stopped to watch the tender scene before him.

Valentina crooned a lullaby to her son as she suckled him and with her hair loose about her shoulders and her breast bare to the searching mouth, she looked to the besotted gaze of her husband much as paintings of the Virgin and Child looked in the great cathedrals of Rome and Florence.

"The meal is ready."

Valentina looked up with a smile. "Your son is greedy. I shall not be long and then we shall eat together."

He caressed her hair softly. "I thought we would never eat together again. When I saw you there all covered in blood..."

Valentina had lain without moving, the body of Camille de Brieur heavy across her, pinning her to the ground for several moments. Then, cries of anguish and the weight was lifted from her, allowing the light of the torches to reveal Valentina, white faced and smothered in blood, to the despairing gaze of Raoul de Baisleon.

He snatched her up into his arms, searching for her wounds, the source of all the blood and she smiled weakly and tried to reassure him.

"Not mine, Monsignor. The blood is not mine."

He would not believe that she was unharmed until he had examined every part of her. Then when it became apparent that, indeed she was unhurt, he laughed and clutched her to him until she could scarcely breathe.

"Monsignor, you will be the death of me if you do not cease crushing my ribs so."

Then his embrace eased and he allowed Eloise to help Valentina to her feet.

She was covered in blood. Camille had bled profusely when Eloise's knife had found its mark and Valentina's clothes had to be cut off and taken away for burning.

Camille's men had fought well. It had taken more than a dozen of Raoul's soldiers to overcome them and only one survived to tell the tale of Camille's plotting. Camille's body was wrapped up hurriedly and stacked with those of her bravos ready for a hasty burial the next morning.

Alain was retrieved from his hiding place and when all was quiet again and the camp had settled down, reaction set in.

Valentina had the shakes. She could not seem to get warm and Raoul clasped her in his arms and pressed small kisses to her face and neck and throat. Wine was heated and he forced her to drink, sipping slowly and trying to control her shudders.

"Remind me not to fall out with your maid at any time in the future. She is far too expert with that knife of hers."

"Thankful I am that she is. Or I would be a dead woman right now."

"She can name her reward. The Lion of France is

at her command and she will not have cause to complain of a lack of gratitude or generosity on my part."

"How could Camille have survived, escaped and followed us all these leagues just for revenge?

"She was mad. I cannot believe that I was ever attracted to her. That I was fool enough to get involved with her. I was warned."

"Well. 'Tis all over now. The way home is clear and the sooner we start out the better. Let us not stop until we are safe within our own walls, no matter how hard the journey."

"Your wish is my command."

The Lion's people came out to welcome their lord home from the moment he crossed into his own lands.

The word spread like wildfire. Not only had the seigneur brought home a wife but a son also.

Raoul carried his son before him on his warhorse. Valentina rode so proudly at his side. Autumn turned the hills and forests into blaze of glory and the people lined the way to the castle gates in a cheering, happy throng. Mothers held up their babies to see and Valentina smiled and waved until she ached.

The welcome continued as noisy and enthusiastic until long into the night.

Eloise was content. Rocking the cradle of the heir of Baisleon with her foot and mending a small shirt for her own son, Charles, she could scarcely believe that she, Eloise, of no other name than that, follower in the tail of many an army for so long, had achieved the position of maid to the Lady de Baisleon. Her man, soon to be her husband, Arnaud, had been made marshal-at-arms here at Baisleon and Eloise carried his child.

Roars of acclaim from the hall below made her smile. She knew that Valentina would retire soon and Raoul would not be far behind her.

In fact, the Lion had already leaned across to whisper in his wife's ear and what he said nobody could hear. Valentina, however, blushed before pushing back her chair and rising to her feet. As she left the hall, Raoul stood and raised his cup to the merry throng at his table.

"My friends, a toast. To my lady wife and to the son she bore me. May we all stay healthy and safe within these walls for many a year to come."

They cheered until they had no more breath and some passed out with the drink and the heat and the excitement. When the cheering had finished, the Lion too, had left the table and followed his wife to bed.

Magic

Magic are your eyes
When you look across at me,
Magic is your voice
When you whisper tenderly.
Magic is the time
We spend silently together,
When you kiss me in the rain
The magic's there forever.
Magic is your warmth
When you hold me in your arms,
You caress my aching body
With your potions and your charms.
Our magic precious nights
When pain turns into pleasure,
Our dreams are now fulfilled —
Our love will last for ever.

Jenny Martin